TREASURED BY THE DRAGON

Stonefire Dragons #13

JESSIE DONOVAN

Mythical Lake Press, LLC

Treasured by the Dragon
Copyright © 2020 Laura Hoak-Kagey
Mythical Lake Press, LLC
First Print Edition

Cover Art by Laura Hoak-Kagey of Mythical Lake Design
ISBN: 978-1944776190

Want to stay up-to-date on releases? Please join my newsletter by clicking here.

Books in this series:

Stonefire Dragons
Sacrificed to the Dragon (SD #1)
Seducing the Dragon (SD #2)
Revealing the Dragons (SD #3)
Healed by the Dragon (SD #4)
Reawakening the Dragon (SD #5)
Loved by the Dragon (SD #6)
Surrendering to the Dragon (SD #7)
Cured by the Dragon (SD #8)
Aiding the Dragon (SD #9)
Finding the Dragon (SD #10)
Craved by the Dragon (SD #11)
Persuading the Dragon (SD #12)
Treasured by the Dragon (SD #13)
Captivating the Dragon / Hayley & Nathan (SD #14, TBD)

Treasured by the Dragon Synopsis

If someone had told Dawn Chadwick that she'd be attending a play put on by children on a dragon-shifter's land a year ago, she would've said they were mad. However, her daughter Daisy has slowly worn Dawn down about her prejudices and she ends up volunteering to help with the play. She's to assist a recluse dragonman with the special effects. What she didn't count on was her daughter's meddling.

Blake Whitby prefers working in a lab to being around people. He's a rare white dragon with a black spot, and the attention from a young age has made him hide from others. However, he's always had a weakness for children and agrees to help them with their play. What he didn't count on was meeting a beautiful human with a sense of humor and a heart-warming smile. His dragon wants her, but Blake holds back. At least until two kids make holding back impossible.

While Dawn agrees to the mate-claim frenzy with Blake, there's no guarantee their pairing will work. And when Dawn's family threatens her happiness, Blake has to stand by his mate and fight for the family he never knew he wanted.

The Stonefire and Lochguard series intertwine with one another. Since so many readers ask for the overall reading order, I've included it with this book. (This list is as of September 2020 and you can view the most up-to-date version on my website at www.JessieDonovan.com)

Sacrificed to the Dragon (Stonefire Dragons #1)
Seducing the Dragon (Stonefire Dragons #2)
Revealing the Dragons (Stonefire Dragons #3)
Healed by the Dragon (Stonefire Dragons #4)
Reawakening the Dragon (Stonefire Dragons #5)
The Dragon's Dilemma (Lochguard Highland Dragons #1)
Loved by the Dragon (Stonefire Dragons #6)
The Dragon Guardian (Lochguard Highland Dragons #2)
Surrendering to the Dragon (Stonefire Dragons #7)
The Dragon's Heart (Lochguard Highland Dragons #3)
Cured by the Dragon (Stonefire Dragons #8)
The Dragon Warrior (Lochguard Highland Dragons #4)
Aiding the Dragon (Stonefire Dragons #9)
Finding the Dragon (Stonefire Dragons #10)
Craved by the Dragon (Stonefire Dragons #11)
The Dragon Family (Lochguard Highland Dragons #5)
Winning Skyhunter (Stonefire Dragons Universe #1)
The Dragon's Discovery (Lochguard Highland Dragons #6)
Transforming Snowridge (Stonefire Dragons Universe #2)
The Dragon's Pursuit (Lochguard Highland Dragons #7)
Persuading the Dragon (Stonefire Dragons #12)
Treasured by the Dragon (Stonefire Dragons #13)

The Dragon Collective (Lochguard Highland Dragons #8, 2021)

Short stories that can be enjoyed any time after *Winning Skyhunter/The Dragon's Discovery*:

Meeting the Humans (Stonefire Dragons Shorts #1)
The Dragon Camp (Stonefire Dragons Shorts #2)
The Dragon Play (Stonefire Dragons Shorts #3)

Semi-related dragon stories set in the USA, beginning sometime around *The Dragon's Discovery / Transforming Snowridge*:

The Dragon's Choice (Tahoe Dragon Mates #1)
The Dragon's Need (Tahoe Dragon Mates #2)
The Dragon's Bidder (Tahoe Dragon Mates #3)
The Dragon's Charge (Tahoe Dragon Mates #4, Nov 2020)
The Dragon's Weakness (Tahoe Dragon Mates #5, 2021)

Chapter One

Dawn Chadwick did her best to drive and sing along to the music playing on the car stereo without thinking about her destination for the evening— a dragon-shifter's clan lands.

A quick glance over at her eleven-year-old daughter, singing and bobbing her head to the music, making strange hand motions in the process, reminded her of why Dawn was driving to Clan Stonefire in the Lake District. Daisy was to be the star of a play featuring both human and dragon-shifter children.

It wasn't the first time her daughter had been to Stonefire. No, earlier in the year, her class had taken a field trip and then later participated in a summer camp of sorts. The first time signing the permission form had been the hardest for Dawn. But in the end, she'd decided it was better to expose her daughter firsthand to the dragon-shifters instead of relying on hearsay like Dawn had done her whole life.

And ever since Daisy had returned from her first field trip to Stonefire, she'd talked nonstop about the dragon-shifters and a new friend she'd made. True, Daisy had gotten up to a bit of mischief during her visit—sneaking off with her new friend to see a Stonefire teenager in his dragon form—but her daughter tended to find trouble on occasion. And Daisy really did try to do better, although her hyper energy levels made it difficult some-times for her to think about the full consequences of her actions.

Daisy required patience in abundance, and lots of love. Some parents couldn't handle children like her daughter, such as her ex-husband and Daisy's father, who'd left them rather than deal with the challenge.

The bastard.

No. Tonight is about Daisy. Nothing else matters.

The song ended and Daisy bounced in her seat. "Since I can't ask are we there yet again or else you'll turn around and drive back to Manchester, how many more times can we play that song before we get there?"

Dawn couldn't help but smile. Daisy was nothing if not inventive when it came to finding loopholes. "Not even one more time. Look up ahead. Do you see those tiny lights in the distance? According to the sat-nav, that should be where Stonefire's front gates are."

Daisy leaned forward. "It's so different in the dark. Not even during the camp did we drive around at night. I wonder if they put up some sort of torches, or special color-changing lights, or something to greet us. That would be way better than regular old lights."

Dawn laughed. "Probably not. After all, we have to save the special stuff for the play, right?"

Daisy leaned back in her seat and tapped her legs with her hands. "That's right. And you're going to help Mr. Whitby with the special effects. He's a little shy, so maybe don't be too stern. Or serious. You can always make me giggle, so maybe you should make Mr. Whitby giggle."

Dawn bit her lip a second before replying, "I don't think dragonmen giggle."

"Oh, I'm sure they do. Freddie's done it before, even if he denies it. They really are just like us, Mum. So don't be afraid. No one will eat you or anything. They're nice."

Through Daisy's enthusiasm, Dawn had learned to give them a chance. Still, seeing a person with flashing dragon eyes would be a little strange to someone like her, who'd never been around a dragon-shifter before. "I'm going to try, Daisy, like I said. Just remember you've spent more time around the dragons than me. I need a bit of time, too, to get to know them."

Daisy bounced a little. "So many of them will be there tonight. You'll get to meet everyone. Mr. MacLeod, Bram, and even Kai, who is the security-type guy who pretends to never smile. But I made him do it once before. So he *does* smile, but only if you're really special."

"Then I'll try to be really special." She rounded a curve in the road and gasped at the site of the giant metal gate, which was lit by a giant flame torch on either side. The word "Stonefire" was on the top of it, spelled out in metal.

Daisy clapped her hands. "See? They do like torches.

Maybe someone heard me asking about them and put them up. I can make more suggestions. If I didn't have to remember all my lines, then I'd try to think of some things to tell Bram. But the lines will be hard enough."

Dawn pulled to a stop in front of the gate. "Don't worry, Daisy-love. You've been trying so hard and practicing constantly. I know you'll do fine."

Before her daughter could reply, the gate opened, and a voice from some speaker said, "Drive inside and take the first left. Park in front of the large building there."

Daisy clapped her hands. "That's the Protector building. It's their fancy word for security. Maybe you'll meet Kai, that serious dragonman. He's really tall, and handsome, but he has a mate. So don't fall in love with him, Mum. His mate won't like it."

She cleared her throat and glanced over at her daughter. "I'll try not to."

Her daughter completely missed Dawn's sarcasm. "Good. Oooh, there he is! Standing right in front of the building. Look at his muscles, Mum. He doesn't need to be in his dragon form to snap someone in half!"

"Daisy Mae, people simply don't snap someone in half."

She parked the car, turned off the ignition, and gently took Daisy's wrist to keep her from bolting from the car. "Now, remember that tonight is special. Everyone is looking forward to the play that you've all worked so hard on. You need to be on your best behavior, like you promised, so that it goes off without a hitch. Okay?"

"I know, Mum. I won't go wandering, I promise."

Even though her daughter tried to follow directions, it didn't always happen.

Still, Dawn smiled, released Daisy's wrist, and said, "Good, because I need you to introduce me to everyone until you have to go get ready for the play. I'll be lost if you disappear."

Daisy's eyes widened. "I can do that, introduce everyone. I've memorized so many people's names. I haven't met them all yet, so maybe I can surprise them. Yes, that will be a fantastic game to play. Keep track for me, okay, Mum? See how many I get right."

She snorted. "I'll do my best. Now, let's not keep the eagle-eyed dragonman waiting."

Daisy undid her seat belt and was out of the car before Dawn could do more than blink. Quickly, she followed suit and caught up to Daisy, who stood in front of the one she'd called Kai.

He was quite tall, hovering at least six inches above Dawn, and wasn't smiling. His eyes appeared to take everything in, and nothing got past him. She didn't know how anyone would want to try and defy him looking like that.

The dragonman was definitely a little intimidating. Dawn hoped some of the others would be less so or her evening would be a long one.

Doing her best to calm her heart rate, she forced a smile and said, "Hello. I'm Dawn Chadwick, Daisy's mum."

The dragonman grunted. "I'm Kai. Now, follow me. I'll take you to the great hall, where everything is happening tonight."

He turned and walked away, clearly expecting them to follow. Daisy whispered loudly, "We have to keep up. Come on, Mum."

Daisy took her hand and pulled her at almost a run. Dawn, never the runner, struggled to keep up.

So much for looking cool and collected for when she encountered nearly an entire dragon clan. She only hoped they understood that being Daisy's mum meant handling everything by the seat of your pants.

BLAKE WHITBY FROWNED at the empty stage as barely a few puffs of smoke erupted. There should've been more, much more, according to his calculations.

His inner dragon—the second personality inside his head—yawned and spoke up. *It's enough smoke for a children's play. I don't know why you're spending so much time on this.*

You're the one who said we needed to get out more. This is me trying, although your other request for finding a mate isn't going to happen.

It doesn't have to be tonight. But tinkering, and calculating, and the other boring rubbish you like so much isn't enough for me. You can have that during the day, but I want sex at night.

Blake mentally sighed. *Again with the sex? Don't you remember what happened last time we tried to find someone to occupy you?*

His beast huffed. *Don't act as if it's merely for me, and it wasn't that bad. You should be happy since I didn't get any sex in the end anyway.*

Right, tell yourself it wasn't embarrassing.

However, it had been that bad. The female had refused to do anything until she could see his dragon form and take a picture.

Which Blake had refused.

He was a white dragon with a black spot, which was extremely rare. Almost like the unicorn of dragons, especially since his black spot was more iridescent than plain black.

Every female—not to mention quite a few males—wanted to see and touch the spot for luck or to make a wish.

Granted, it was better than when he'd been younger and everyone had teased him for it, calling it the dirty spot.

To avoid the attention, both good and bad, Blake preferred working by himself and living alone in a small cabin just outside Stonefire's main living area.

Only because he loved volunteering with the children at school, hoping to encourage them to study the sciences, had he ended up helping with the children's play.

Which meant he needed to get it right. Especially since he'd been paired with a human volunteer who would probably be of no help at all.

His dragon grunted. *Stop assuming the worst. Just tinker with whatever you need to make more smoke come out, and then it'll give us more time to peruse all the human females coming tonight. They won't care about our spot or want to touch it for luck. It can just be sex, and more sex, until we pass out.*

With a sigh, Blake walked back toward the small area

being used as his base for controlling the special effects. *We can fly and hunt tomorrow instead. You like that.*

If we do any more of that, I'll be too fat to fly soon.

I don't want to talk about this anymore. Now, be quiet so I can finish this on time. Otherwise, we'll disappoint the children.

Since inner dragons treasured children, it was one way to get his beast to stop talking about mates and sex. *Fine. But once the play is over, I'll be back.*

Blake doubted his dragon would stay silent that long, but he didn't argue.

He retreated to the room being used to control the special effects. As he adjusted the various settings, time flew by. Only when Tristan MacLeod's voice—he was one of the teachers in charge of the play—blared from the in-room speaker did he snap out of it. "Blake, your human volunteer is here. Come meet her in the great hall."

Since the speaker system in the small room wasn't two-way, Blake reluctantly turned from his computer and exited the room. It'd been a long time since he'd met an adult human who wasn't mated to one of his clan members. Some of them went lust-crazy over dragon-shifters. Even if Blake wasn't the fittest of the males on Stonefire, he did his fair share of flying and had enough muscles.

Not that he cared. They seemed to attract unwanted human notice.

His dragon grunted. *Good. Dragons like attention. I wish you'd embrace it.*

Blake picked up his pace until he reached the small door that exited into the biggest room inside the great hall. As he hovered there, he scanned the crowd for the little human girl named Daisy—it was her mother he was to work with—and finally spotted her curly blonde hair. Someone was in the way of the adult with her, but they finally moved, and Blake drew in a breath.

Daisy's mother had lovely blonde hair to her chin, a smile that could warm any dreary day, and a little experience in her gaze that told him she wasn't some brainless teenager looking for a quick score.

His beast huffed. *Then go talk to her.*

His dragon's words snapped Blake out of his trance. *I will. But just because she's pretty doesn't mean anything. She's Daisy's mother, and I won't risk hurting her. Not when that human child seems to be so important to all the dragon teachers and Bram.*

Why do you assume we'd hurt her?

I don't have time for a ready-made family. We're on the verge of a breakthrough in our latest project, which will help protect the dragon-shifters.

There's no reason we can't do all of it, both the work and a family. It's not as if you can work twenty-four hours a day.

Not wanting to go in circles, Blake ignored his beast, stood tall, and walked toward Daisy and her mother. The best way to make it all go quicker was to pretend he hadn't seen the humans. That way they'd think him aloof and maybe dissuade them from conversation. Blake wouldn't be rude, but he wasn't going to encourage anyone, either.

And so Blake was careful to keep his glance only on Freddie, one of the young male dragon-shifters, and the boy's mother as he made his way toward them.

Dawn had just finished meeting Daisy's best friend on Stonefire—a boy named Freddie Atherton—when another tall dragonman with light brown hair, pale skin, and hazel eyes marched up to them. He looked straight at Freddie and asked, "We need to get a move on or we'll be late. Did the human parents arrive yet?"

Dawn was about to say something when Freddie gestured toward her. "Daisy's mum is here. She's going to help you."

The man's gaze followed Freddie's finger pointing at her, and the dragonman looked at Dawn's face. His eyes were inquisitive and focused, as if memorizing her features. Then his pupils flashed to slits and back to round, and Dawn couldn't hold back a gasp as she stumbled backward.

She'd never seen the changing pupils before, and they really did turn into a reptilian-type shape. If she remembered right, it meant the dragon half was talking whenever that happened.

Her daughter tugged her hand. "Don't be afraid, Mum. It's just his dragon half. It's like his best friend, always there, talking and giving advice. Not always good advice, but they mean well. And Mr. Whitby's really nice. He's not going to shift and shred you to pieces."

Daisy's words snapped Mr. Whitby's attention, and he frowned. "Of course not. No one on Stonefire would do that unless someone hurt or killed one of our own."

Daisy bobbed her head. "See? You'll be fine, Mum. And Mr. Whitby's brilliant. He made some special things for our play. He didn't have to, but he did. So make sure to be careful and not drop and break something."

Her daughter's words brought Dawn back to the present and stated, "Daisy Mae, I don't break things."

"Sometimes you do. You say that's where I get it from. You say it all the time, Mum. Remember?"

Dawn's cheeks heated. It really shouldn't matter since she'd only see the dragonman for the evening and go home. But still, no one liked having their faults shouted to the world at the first opportunity.

Willing her cheeks to cool, Dawn cleared her throat. "We'll talk about this after the play. Will you be all right if I go help Mr. Whitby?"

Mr. Whitby spoke up, his voice somewhat calmer and gentler than before. "Call me Blake. And she'll be fine. The great hall is one of the safest places on the clan."

Daisy shifted from one foot to the other, her actions telling Dawn that she wanted to go have fun with her friend. Only because an entire dragon clan was watching over the human children tonight did she not comment and give another reminder.

Daisy motioned toward the door. "Go, Mum. I'll see you after the show."

Dawn shared a glance with Freddie's mother, Sasha, who stood nearby—the dragonwoman confirming with a look that she'd keep her eye on Daisy—and then nodded. "Okay. Do your best tonight, Daisy. I'll be filming it all to show everyone."

Once Daisy bobbed her head, Dawn finally turned toward Blake. He stared at her, studying her face as if he'd just seen it for the first time all over again.

She almost asked if she had something on her cheek or nose, but decided not to. Daisy had already embarrassed her once, and she didn't need to encourage any more. "What do I need to do?"

With a grunt, Blake turned and motioned toward a door on the far side of the room. "Follow me and we'll get started."

Every cell in Dawn's body urged her to look back and ensure Daisy was okay. But her daughter had turned eleven the day before and was no longer a baby. Dawn was trying to give her a little more responsibility and trust.

Besides, Freddie's mother would look after them. They'd had several phone conversations since the dragon camp, and Sasha Atherton was probably the closest thing to a friend she had on Stonefire.

Although right before Dawn entered the door, she did steal a quick glance only to find Daisy laughing. The sight warmed her heart and gave her the courage to leave her daughter in the care of others for a short while.

So she entered the door, followed Blake Whitby, and waited to see what she needed to do for the night.

Chapter Two

B lake somehow kept his emotions in check as he guided Dawn through the door into the backstage area.

His dragon growled. *How can you be so calm? She's our true mate. I can tell. She should be ours.*

Of all the females in the world, what were the chances he'd meet his true mate at a play for children?

It wasn't as if he didn't think she was beautiful. But he knew nothing about her besides the fact she had a daughter.

And that fact alone could interrupt his plans to help protect the clan from dragon hunters and Dragon Knights. They'd received some data from the Dragon Knights, brought by a human who was a former Knight herself, which had helped tremendously. However, there were still quite a few gaps he needed to work out.

His dragon spoke up again. *You can't spend all your*

bloody time on the project. Besides, it would be nice to have some company in our cabin.

Even putting aside my own wants, you saw how she was afraid of our flashing eyes. I don't have time for an energetic daughter and a fearful mate.

For now, just be nice to her. You never know, once you get to know her, then maybe you'll want her like I do.

Dawn's voice came from behind him. "It's nice of you to help the children this way. From what I heard from Daisy, you usually don't like crowds."

"Not usually." He stopped in front of a table loaded with unused smoke canisters and confetti cartridges packed securely in boxes and finally faced her. "But it's pretty hard to say no to a whole group of kids."

She smiled, and his heart rate kicked up. If she'd been beautiful to him before, she was bloody gorgeous now. "Do you really mean it's hard to say no to Daisy?"

He couldn't help but smile back. "She is persistent."

"That's the nicest way to say it. But she has a good heart."

Blake heard some whispering and caught sight of Daisy and Freddie sneaking away. They must've come backstage after Dawn.

Once they were out of earshot, he nodded. "She does. Although for a human, she's nearly as curious as an inner dragon can be at times. I imagine that's why she gets along so well with Freddie and most of the other dragon-shifter children. She's human, but not quite."

As soon as the words left his lips, he wanted to kick himself. His words could be construed as an insult, which was not his plan. Even if he didn't want a mate, he didn't need to be rude to Dawn.

Dawn tilted her head, her straight hair brushing her shoulder, banishing any other thoughts unrelated to her. He itched to reach out and see if it was as soft as he imagined.

He nearly blinked. Blake usually didn't pay attention to such things, but it was almost as if he couldn't ignore Dawn, even if he wanted to.

His dragon snorted. *Good.*

Blake half expected Dawn to take a step back again since his pupils would've flashed when his dragon spoke, but she held her ground. Tucking a section of hair behind her ear, she asked, "What's it like, talking with someone inside your head all the time?"

He shrugged one shoulder. "Pretty much like Daisy explained it, with one caveat—they can be really annoying at times. And yet, I can't imagine my life without him."

"It must be nice then, to never be alone."

A brief flicker of sadness came across Dawn's eyes, but it was gone in the next instant. And while there was still a lot to do before the show, he couldn't just ignore the look. "You have your daughter."

"Oh, of course. I love Daisy more than anything. But I imagine your dragon ages at the same rate as you, right? And talking with someone your own age isn't quite the same as having conversations with a child."

Blake paused, wondering if he should ask some more personal questions. His dragon growled. *Don't hold back with her. No matter what you foolishly think right now, she's our true mate. Give her a chance.*

And for once, Blake didn't dismiss his dragon's prodding. He asked, "What happened to Daisy's father?"

For a few beats, Dawn remained silent, and Blake wondered if he'd fucked up. Since he didn't spend a lot of time around other people, he wasn't exactly the best at social niceties. Still, why shouldn't he ask about such an important part of her life? He'd never be able to get to know the human and slightly appease his beast otherwise.

Dawn finally sighed, ending the awkward silence. "He left a long time ago and lives in Australia." She paused a second, and Blake sensed he should stay quiet. He was rewarded when she added, "After all the infertility issues we had, he was already stressed. In the end, Daisy was too much for him to handle as a toddler, and he left."

Blake clenched his fingers into a fist. Scientist he may be, but he was still a dragon-shifter, and his kind tended to treasure family, no matter the challenges. "Then he's a bloody idiot."

Dawn blinked. "Yes, he is."

He nearly reached out a hand to smooth some hair back from her face but resisted. Touching his true mate would only drive his inner beast crazy, and he couldn't risk it.

His dragon harrumphed, but Blake spoke up before his beast could comment. "For all Daisy's chatter, she's never talked about her father that I can recall. So I'm guessing he's gone for good?"

Dawn smiled sadly and bobbed her head. "He felt

leaving her when she was still young would be best. I haven't heard from him in years, and at this point, I don't want to. The only connection I have to him is his sister, who's tried to get to know Daisy a little. But that's it."

His dragon hissed. *The fucker. Daisy deserves better. We could do better.*

Instead of answering his beast, Blake focused on Dawn. "Well, just know that if he were a dragonman, then I would challenge him for what he did to you and Daisy. Bram would've kicked him out of the clan, for sure, if he'd refused to take care of his child."

Probably. But for some reason, it was important for Blake to say those words right now.

His dragon said softly, *Because you're starting to want her, too.*

The human female tilted her head. "Your dragon is talking again."

"Like always. He rarely stays quiet. Let's just say he's not a fan of your ex, either."

She hesitated a second before asking, "Do you ever show your dragon to humans?"

Blake's first response was to shut down, dismiss her, and walk away.

Then he remembered that Dawn knew nothing about the color of his dragonhide, let alone about the spot. She was merely curious. "Not usually."

"Oh," she said as her shoulders slumped ever so slightly.

His dragon growled. *She should get to see us. Tell her.*

And for some reason, he didn't feel the urge to fight

his beast. "But maybe for you I can make a special case and show you at some point, if you like."

Her eyes lit up, reminding him a little of Daisy. No one could doubt they were mother and daughter.

Dawn said, "Really? Maybe I should be the adult and say it's no big deal, but I think every human wonders about seeing a dragon-shifter in their dragon form at some point. A year ago, I never would've thought it possible. But Daisy changed all that, partly through her sheer force of will."

He grinned. "Yes, she can be convincing. I think she might end up being the Department of Dragon Affairs director at some point in the future."

Dawn shook her head. "I doubt she'd last long enough through the bureaucracy to do that. But I can easily see her forming her own group, touring the UK and Ireland, and singlehandedly trying to change every-one's opinion about dragon-shifters."

"She just might," he replied.

As they smiled at one another yet again—Blake couldn't remember the last time he'd smiled so much around another person—a pent-up longing rushed through his body. Not merely because his true mate stood before him. No, it was more than that. He'd been mostly alone since his mother had died a few years back, and always denied any shred of loneliness.

Dawn made him wonder if he wanted a mate after all.

His dragon spoke up. *I told you not to spend so much time in isolation. But it worked out in the end since it meant we waited for our true mate to show up.*

Blake resisted saying his dragon was right for fear of stoking his ego too much.

However, he noticed the change in Dawn's reaction to his flashing eyes. The fact Dawn didn't so much as blink now told him how much she'd overcome her fear already.

Maybe, just maybe, if he took things slow, he might try to know her better.

His dragon hummed. *Yes, yes, I like that idea. And now I won't let you run away from her, either.*

Just as he was about to reply, one of the dragon teachers—Ella Lawson—walked up to them and asked, "Is everything set for the play? We'll be starting in half an hour."

Blake cleared his throat. "Nearly there. We're just on our way to load the special effects items and go to the control room."

Ella nodded. "Good." She handed him a walkie-talkie. "We'll communicate this way. Now, excuse me, I need to make sure the children aren't swapping costumes and doing who knows what with the props. Tristan may think he sees all, but I doubt it when that many kids are in one room together."

As the dragonwoman walked away, Blake handed Dawn the walkie-talkie. When his fingers brushed hers, electricity rushed up his arm and he sucked in a breath.

He heard Dawn do the same.

They stared at one another for a few beats, and for the first time in his adult life, Blake nearly lost control and kissed the human.

Good. Just try to kiss her. Look, she just bit her bottom lip. She's probably thinking about it, too.

No, dragon, no kissing. She doesn't know all the facts, and I won't hide what could happen from her. If flashing eyes startled her, then a mate-claim frenzy would send her running away for good.

Before his beast could reply, he removed his hand and motioned for Dawn to follow. "Come on. We don't have a lot of time to finish setting everything up."

And once they reached the stage to place the final few things for the show, Blake was attuned to Dawn as she moved about the area.

There were so many reasons he should end the night and pretend he'd never met her. After all, the clan was counting on him to help crack some of the Dragon Knight data they'd received, data that would help Stone-fire defend themselves against one of their main human enemies.

And yet, part of him wondered if he could handle his work as well as a mate, a child, and another on the way since a frenzy always resulted in pregnancy.

Maybe if he solved the last of the puzzles to defeat the Dragon Knights, he'd have enough time.

Despite his intentions for the evening, it seemed like his life had changed after all. The only question was how he could handle it going forward.

Chapter Three

As Dawn stood behind the curtain at the side of the stage and watched the closing scenes of the play— her daughter playing the part of an old dragon-shifter queen of Britain—she couldn't stop smiling.

Daisy had done much better than she could've antici- pated. Maybe acting was something she was destined to do. The fact Daisy had only forgotten maybe two lines was a massive deal for her daughter since her attention wavered a lot.

As the lights dimmed, Dawn clapped as loud as she could, loving how the children bowed to the crowd.

True, she'd hoped to sit in the audience, but Blake had needed her help to move things around as the play progressed. And considering she'd wanted it to be the best it could be for Daisy's debut, she'd merely ensured that Sasha recorded it all for her.

As the kids dragged out the teachers so they could also bow to the audience, Dawn hurried back toward the small control room where Blake would be. Even though her night was over, and she still needed to congratulate Daisy, she wanted to see him one more time. Given that all the teachers wanted the kids out of their costumes before being reunited with their parents—some of the fake dragon wings were pointy, and no one wanted to take chances—she should have enough time to say goodbye to him.

Dawn weaved through the maze of props and other adults moving about. She reached the outer door to the room divided in two, and paused to smooth her hair. It was silly, really, to worry about her appearance. But something about Blake made her feel like the nineteen-year-old version of herself, back when boys had made her belly flip and cheeks heat up.

Taking a deep breath, she entered the outer room and then the inner one. Blake turned toward her and smiled. She loved how his eyes crinkled at the corners. It was so much better than when he tried to be solemn and quiet.

She shut the door and went over to him. "It all went brilliantly, Blake. Nothing caught fire and everything went off when it was supposed to."

He said dryly, "Those are some pretty low standards."

Snorting, she playfully touched his arm. "In my book, not starting a fire is a pretty important deal. Especially with a stage full of children, half of whom were wearing flammable wings."

Blake's pupils flashed a few times between round and slitted. But Dawn didn't pay much attention to them since it was almost normal to her now.

When he took her hand in his, she completely forgot about everything but the man in front of her. Time seemed to stand still.

She couldn't remember the last time a man's touch had turned her brain to mush and filled her with warmth and anticipation.

Not that anything would happen. Did she want to see Blake again? Yes. But Dawn had to be careful because of Daisy. Her daughter became attached rather easily, and Dawn didn't want to dangle anything in front of Daisy before Dawn knew something could be serious.

Why am I even thinking about stuff like that? I just met the man.

He released her hand and said, "I think most of the students were extra careful so as to not irk Tristan. He's good with the children for many reasons, but they instinctively know not to piss him off."

She smiled, remembering the usually growly dragonman when he'd talked with his mate briefly during the intermission. He'd been cooing to his small daughter the entire time. "I think it's more than that, though. He hides a good heart, although I'm not sure why."

"Image, maybe? Most dragon-shifter males—and quite a few females—like to project an alpha persona."

She raised an eyebrow. "What, and you're different?"

His gaze shuttered a second, but it vanished before she could blink. "In many ways, yes."

She searched his eyes but decided now wasn't the time to push for the reason behind the change in his expression. Daisy would be looking for her any minute now, and Dawn sensed the conversation behind Blake's demeanor required more than a few rushed seconds.

So she decided to let it drop and changed the subject. "Well, regardless, you did a good job, Blake. Oh, and give your dragon a pat on the back for me."

He raised his brows. "My dragon?"

"I assume he helped you, right? And I can't really talk to him right now, so I have to use you as the messenger."

Blake's eyes flashed as he snorted. "My dragon doesn't care much for science-y stuff, as he calls it."

Interesting. Maybe she had just enough time to learn a little more about how inner dragons worked. For Daisy, of course. Not because Dawn was getting more and more interested in Blake Whitby by the second. "So you and your dragon like different things?"

He shrugged. "Sometimes, and other times it's the same. We both like swimming, for example."

She smiled. "Does that mean you float on your back in the lake, shifting into your dragon form for a short while, and then switch back to your human one?"

He chuckled. "Can't say I've tried it that way, but it might be worth a go. I'll just have to make sure there aren't any humans around since I have to be naked to do that."

She laughed. "That would be quite the show, for sure. And since almost every mobile phone can record video, it might become the next viral video. Naked dragonman on vacation, or something."

As they smiled at each other, Dawn craved more of this—easy conversation and teasing with a man. And not just some random man, but one who already knew her daughter and all that could entail if things went well.

However, before she could brush those thoughts from her mind, someone pushed her from behind, and she crashed into Blake, her lips touching his.

Despite the unexpected kiss, the brief touch sent heat rushing through her body, more than she'd ever felt before.

But in the next beat, Blake pushed her away, took a few steps back, and clutched his head in his hands. His eyes were shut and his jaw also looked clenched.

If she didn't know any better, she'd say he looked in pain. Dawn reached for him. "Blake, are you okay?"

He shoved her hand away. "No, get away from me, Dawn. Run. Now."

As he hunched over and hissed, Dawn didn't know what to do. Something was clearly wrong with Blake. Maybe it had to do with his inner dragon?

Just as she contemplated getting help, Freddie whispered, "It's the mate-claim frenzy, right?"

She barely noted Freddie and Daisy were also in the room. What was a mate-claim frenzy? Dawn had no idea.

Before she could ask, Blake's eyes shot to the boy's. "Yes, now get them out of here and find Bram, Kai, someone." The dragonman crouched down into a ball on the floor. "Hurry."

As he moaned in pain, Dawn decided enough was enough. Inner dragon or not, she couldn't let him suffer. She moved to crouch down, but Freddie rushed to stand between them. The little boy stated, "Don't touch him. It'll make it worse."

She frowned. Freddie didn't speak often, and never with such conviction before. "What's going on—"

Freddie cut Dawn off. "We need to leave. Bram will explain it to you."

Even though she'd just met Blake, the sight of him curled into himself did something to her heart.

Had she caused this? They'd talked all evening with no problem. The only thing different had been the accidental kiss.

Not that she felt asking Freddie would be the best idea. Maybe she did need to talk with the clan leader.

However, before she could ask Freddie to take her, the little dragon boy took her hand, and she let him lead her out of the room. When she glanced one last time at Blake curled on the floor, Dawn noticed Daisy followed silently behind her, too.

It seemed even her daughter sensed something had just happened, even if she had no bloody idea what a mere kiss could do to a strong dragonman like Blake.

Once they were outside of the special set of rooms, Freddie released Dawn's hand and said firmly, "Don't go in there. We need to find some help."

"Why?" Daisy asked.

"Because Mr. Whitby's dragon wants your mum, and soon will do anything to have her, even if it means fighting off other males to get her."

The image of Blake fighting off other dragonmen to get to her made the blood drain from her face. It was hard to reconcile that idea with the slightly shy, gentle man with hidden humor from earlier. But there was so much about dragon-shifters she didn't know.

Maybe there was a side to dragon-shifters that was the root of all the rumors and whispers she'd heard over the years.

The familiar voice of Tristan MacLeod reached her ears, bringing her back to the present. "Here you two are. Now, come on."

Freddie rushed to the teacher. "No, wait, listen. Mr. Whitby and Daisy's mum kissed, and now he's trying to fight his dragon against the mate-claim frenzy. He's in there." He pointed. "Help him."

Tristan muttered, "Bloody fucking hell," before rushing to the door. "Do as the boy says, Dawn. Follow him. You need to see Bram straightaway."

Dawn glanced one last time at the door, wondering what would happen to Blake. She hoped nothing horrible because his pain was her fault in a way. Freddie implied it was the kiss that had changed everything. And if Daisy hadn't pushed her into him, then none of this would've happened.

You need more information, Dawn. So go get it. With a deep breath, she looked back at Freddie. The boy stood taller and motioned for them to follow him.

She barely noticed the walk to the great hall, only aware of Daisy taking her hand. Since her daughter didn't do that often anymore, the touch helped calm Dawn's thumping heart. She forced a small smile down at Daisy, a little worried at how quiet she was.

However, she didn't get to ask Daisy anything since they exited the door and entered the great hall. Tristan must've called Bram because he and his mate—she couldn't remember the woman's name—waited for them.

Bram's face was expressionless, his eyes assessing her as they stopped. He was so much taller than Blake, and a lot more intimidating. This man held control over an entire clan of dragon-shifters.

Then his pale-skinned, ginger-haired mate stepped in front of Bram and smiled. She said, "We met briefly earlier, but I'm Evie, Bram's mate. I'm a human just like you."

Dawn looked between Evie, Bram, and back again. Time to push aside any fears and get some bloody answers. "What's going on? Everyone keeps saying you'll explain it all to me, and that just makes me even more worried."

"We'll explain it all in just a moment." Evie glanced down at Freddie. "Why don't you take Daisy to the party and stay close to your family? Can you do that?"

Daisy frowned. "I want to hear what's going on, too."

Bram spoke up. "Not right now, little one. Freddie can tell you what's happening. But we need to have an adults-only conversation with your mother."

Dawn knew how much Daisy hated "adults-only" conversations. But before she could tell Daisy to go with Freddie, the boy took Daisy's hand and said, "I can take her to my family. And we'll watch over her, Mrs. Chadwick. I promise."

Freddie really was a sweet boy.

She looked down at her daughter and tucked a stray strand of hair behind her ear. "Go with Freddie and stay with his family. I'll find you when I'm done."

"But, Mum."

"No buts, Daisy. Just promise me you won't go looking for any more trouble, okay?"

Daisy must've sensed Dawn's uneasiness because she didn't argue. "Okay. I promise."

She leaned down and kissed Daisy's cheek, the familiar touch helping to calm her a little more. "I'll find you soon."

Daisy glanced from her to Bram, to Bram's mate, and back again. "Okay. I hope it doesn't take too long."

Dawn swore she heard the clan leader murmur, "That depends." However, Freddie pulled Daisy away before she could utter another word.

Taking a deep breath, Dawn met the Stonefire leader's gaze again. "Now what?"

Evie looped her arm through Dawn's. "Let's go to a private room and we'll explain it all, okay?"

She could do nothing but nod and let Evie guide her away, Bram following right on their heels.

It was time to figure out what a bloody mate-claim frenzy entailed and see how her life and Daisy's might change going forward. Because what had happened was probably her fault, and Dawn needed to make it right.

Chapter Four

When Dawn finally sat down at a table, across from Bram and Evie, she did her best not to slump in the chair. She doubted they cared about proper posture, but sitting upright helped Dawn keep it together, too.

And she needed to keep it together because this conversation was probably going to change her life in more ways than one.

Bram shared a look with Evie, and his mate nodded back. The short exchange told Dawn volumes about their relationship. The pair were equals, it seemed, despite the fact Bram could dominate any human if he wanted to.

It was Evie who spoke up first. "What you may not know about me, Dawn, is that I used to work for the DDA before I became Bram's mate."

The DDA—the Department of Dragon Affairs—was a section of the British government that both oversaw dragon-shifters and ran the human sacrifice program.

Dawn didn't know much more than basics of what they did, though.

Evie continued, "I only tell you this because you might need my help once Bram explains everything."

Tired of how they kept beating around the bush, Dawn said, "Then tell me what's going on that may require your help, please. I'm fairly patient, but it's starting to wear thin."

Bram snorted, which made Dawn blink. The drag-onman said, "Well, you're not afraid to tell us what's what, which is a good sign." Dawn unexpectedly growled, and he put up a hand. "Right, then, let's get to the details.

"I don't know the full story behind the kiss, but when your lips touched Blake's, it set off a mate-claim frenzy. What that means is Blake's dragon wants to claim you, their true mate, and have sex with you until you're pregnant."

She blinked. "I—pardon?"

Evie piped up. "Think of it as a nonstop sex marathon with the human form of Blake until you're pregnant. And don't worry, his dragon will be able to tell when you've finally conceived because his scent will end up mixed with yours. I'm sure a scientist could explain that a lot better than me, but trust me, the dragon half will know. The frenzy won't go on forever."

It won't go on forever. But couldn't it if someone couldn't have a baby? Conceiving Daisy had taken Dawn almost four years.

Realizing her jaw had dropped, Dawn promptly closed it. She had so many questions. But since she had no idea how long this meeting would last, she asked the first that came to mind. "Putting aside the sex marathon, as you call it, I don't know what being a true mate means. Is that something Blake would've known?"

Bram nodded and grunted. "Aye, he should've. So let me be blunt—did he kiss you without telling you?"

Something about Bram's tone of voice compelled her to answer. "No, no, that's not what happened." She paused, not wanting to get the kids in trouble but decided she needed to be truthful. If Bram threatened Daisy, then Dawn would stand up to him again. "One of the kids must've tripped or pushed me into Blake. The kiss was accidental."

Bram muttered something she couldn't hear. Evie placed a hand on his arm, and he sighed before saying, "Regardless of how it happened, it's done. There are really only three options in this situation, Dawn. And as much as I hate to rush you, you'll have to pick one fairly soon."

Ignoring the churning in her stomach, she tapped the table. "Then tell me what they are."

"Well, you go through with the frenzy—the sex marathon—and it'll soothe Blake's dragon. Once the baby is born, you can either stay permanently on Stone-fire or leave the baby here and flee. The third option is to leave tonight and stay far away from my clan for the next couple of years, until Blake's dragon is calm enough not to chase after you. And yes, that will mean Daisy will have to keep her distance, too. Blake would never hurt her, but she's a part of you, and it would torture his inner beast to know you were still so close but out of reach."

Dawn tried to process everything Bram had just told her.

To take Daisy away from Stonefire, and Freddie, would devastate her daughter. On top of that, being involved with the dragon-shifters was the first long-term interest Daisy had ever held. While that might not be important for some parents, having a dedicated interest had helped her daughter focus beyond anything Dawn or the schools had been able to accomplish. It was almost as if Daisy tried her best to finish things so she could spend more time learning about the dragons or writing letters to Freddie.

If all of that wasn't enough, Dawn already felt guilty that Daisy didn't have a father. To take away the dragons from her would be almost cruel.

As for herself, it wasn't as if Dawn didn't fancy Blake. She didn't love him, but she had a small connection that could possibly become more. Of course there was one thing that kept her from saying yes.

Something that may tear the dragons away from her daughter anyway.

Doing her best not to dredge up painful memories, Dawn swallowed and said softly, "I probably can't have any more children. So I'm not sure I have any other option but to flee."

Evie asked gently, "What do you mean?"

She met the other woman's gaze and was glad to find kindness instead of pity there. It gave her the courage to extrapolate. "It took nearly four years of IVF treatments to conceive Daisy. She's my little miracle. And so if I said yes to the frenzy, it would probably never end. So I don't know if I really have a choice in the matter."

Evie smiled slightly. "Wonderful things happen between true mates, things you never thought possible. And before you say I'm full of shit, just listen—I was tested at an early age and found out that I was incompatible with dragon-shifters. That's a fancy way of saying I could never have a child with one." Evie placed a hand on her abdomen. "But this isn't my first with Bram, and it's because we're true mates that it happened."

Bram spoke up. "It's true, Dawn. I was told that I was pretty much infertile as well. But it only took finding Evie to make that 1 percent chance a reality several times over."

The pair smiled at each other, but Dawn barely noticed as she tried to wrap her head around what they'd told her.

If it was true, Dawn could have another baby. And most likely without years of hoping and trying to see if something worked.

A longing she'd pent up for more than a decade broke free. She'd always wanted more than one child but had been content with Daisy. No, more than content—she loved her daughter dearly. Dawn simply couldn't imagine her life without her.

But now the dragon-shifters were all but offering her a guaranteed way to have at least one more.

If it were only her, she would instantly say yes and agree to a frenzy.

However, it wasn't just her. If she said yes to Blake, more than one life would change. In other words, Dawn needed to talk with Daisy. And, somehow, she needed to see if she could chat with Blake as well.

Pushing aside her longing, she cleared her throat and garnered the pair's attention. "Thank you for telling me that. I want to say yes, and I know you need an answer soon, but I really do need to speak with Daisy first. And, if there's a way to do it without him going crazy, with Blake, too."

Bram nodded. "Of course you need to talk with your daughter. As for Blake, his dragon will be drugged silent for three days. That's all I can give you before you have to decide one way or the other because if we drug him any longer than that, there can be serious side effects."

She blinked. "You drugged his dragon?"

Bram grunted. "It's the only way to keep him from breaking free and finding you. The inner dragon is far more instinctual than the human half. And when it comes to finding a true mate and claiming them for the frenzy, it can get bloody dangerous."

Evie frowned at Bram before adding, "Don't scare her, Bram." Evie looked at her. "Blake won't be dangerous for the next three days. He's being kept in the surgery and will be carefully monitored. You'll be free to talk with him as much as you need provided you don't touch him. Sometimes, although rare, it can wake the drugged beast early."

"Which means I have less than three days to decide what to do," she stated.

Bram replied, "Aye, that's it. Whatever your decision is, just know that Evie and I will be here to help you along the way. If needed, you can even stay with us for a few days if you want to better know Blake. Provided your talk with Daisy goes well, of course."

Even though the pair seemed nice, she only really knew one person on Stonefire. "You're kind, but if I do remain on Stonefire—which I don't know for sure yet—what about me staying with Sasha Atherton? We've chatted a lot on the phone and it might be easier to stay with her. Then I won't be in the way."

Bram opened his mouth to say something, but Evie beat him to it. "Of course you could stay with Sasha. But just know that we're here whenever you need it, Dawn. If, in the end, you want to live permanently on Stonefire, then I'll find a way to make it happen with the DDA."

Bram smiled. "It's true. Evie has a way with the DDA that's come in quite handy."

She glanced at one face and then the other. If she did stay on Stonefire, it seemed she needed to learn a lot more about the DDA than its name and bare minimum of its duties.

Dawn finally replied, "Okay. Let me talk with Daisy first, and then I'll let you know if I need to see Blake."

The pair stood and Dawn followed suit. Bram opened the door. "Then let's fetch Daisy. You can use this room again for your chat with her."

As they walked down the corridor toward the great hall, Dawn's heart beat double-time and her palms sweated a little. Never in a million years would she have guessed that she would talk with her daughter about living with a dragon clan.

Of course, Dawn had a feeling that Daisy would jump at the chance to live on Stonefire.

And if so, the harder part would be talking with Blake to see if she could envision a future with him. Because if he showed the slightest reluctance about Daisy, Dawn would have to reject the frenzy and flee.

Daisy was her whole world, and even when faced with the greatest temptation of having another baby, Dawn would always put her daughter first.

So she did her best to pack away all her questions and uneasiness about the future to better face her daughter and the difficult conversation ahead.

Chapter Five

As soon as Dawn walked into the great hall, she spotted Daisy's curly blonde head on the far side. Her daughter instantly handed her plate to Freddie in mid-conversation and ran across the room straight toward her.

Dawn did her best to smile and keep Daisy from worrying. As soon as Daisy stopped right in front of her, she met her gaze and asked, "Well? What's going to happen? Are you going with Mr. Whitby?"

Bram frowned down at her. "Just what did Freddie say?"

Daisy shrugged. "Not much. But mate-claim frenzies mean two adults disappear for a bit. And afterward, they have a baby. Is that what you're going to do, Mum? Is it?"

She wished it was as easy as that—Daisy being excited to live on Stonefire and have a sibling. However, her daughter probably didn't understand just how much her life would change. Dawn always tried to be as honest as she could with her daughter, and she wasn't about to change tactics now.

They needed to have a serious chat, end of story.

Dawn took Daisy's hand. "Come, Daisy. We need to talk privately."

Bram motioned back to where they'd come from. "Feel free to use the same room, Dawn."

"Thanks," she murmured before guiding her and Daisy back through the door she'd just came from.

Since Daisy remained silent the entire walk to the room, her daughter must know how serious things were.

A small part of Dawn hated that she'd have to put such a consequential decision before Daisy, but there wasn't any other way. Especially if Dawn wanted to at least try with Blake.

Once they entered the room she'd used with Bram, Dawn sat in one chair and turned another to face her. She motioned toward the empty chair.

Daisy slowly slid into it and asked, "What's going to happen, Mum?"

"I'm not sure yet, Daisy." Her daughter opened her mouth to say more, but Dawn beat her to it. "I wanted to talk with you first before making any decisions."

Daisy scooted forward in her seat. "But you know what I want, Mum. I've always wanted to live here, and I know you always wanted another baby. I thought you'd be excited."

Dawn searched her daughter's eyes and asked something that had been on her mind since finding out about the mate-claim frenzy and all that it entailed. "Did you know that Mr. Whitby was my true mate all along?"

Shaking her head, Daisy's hair bounced back and forth. "No. I just thought you were getting along, and both of you were smiling, and that maybe a kiss would help. Like it always does in the movies."

Right, like the movies. If only it were that easy in real life.

Dawn rubbed her forehead a second before deciding on honesty. "This is a bit more complicated, Daisy. I know how much you love dragon-shifters. And I'm glad you made friends with Freddie. However, I'm still a little afraid of them. Not to mention moving here would mean never seeing Lucy or your other friends at school."

Daisy swung her feet above the ground. "I'll miss Lucy, and I'll always want to see her. But, well, you know, she hasn't been talking to me as much ever since my first visit to Stonefire."

Dawn nearly blinked. Lucy and Daisy had been inseparable for years. Instead, she frowned and asked, "What?"

Daisy looked down at her dress and picked at the skirt. "I didn't tell you because I was trying to fix it. But Lucy's mum told me to not talk to her anymore."

Fury roiled in Dawn's stomach. The fact Connie—Lucy's mother—hadn't even thought of talking to Dawn about something so important made her want to call her up and demand why. Not only because Dawn thought they were friends of a sort, but also because Connie was fully aware of how certain drastic changes could negatively affect Daisy.

And to tell Daisy not to talk with Lucy was also the cowardly way out. Dawn was nice and friendly most of the time, but if someone mistreated her daughter, her temper flared spectacularly. Connie probably knew that and didn't want the confrontation.

Her emotions must've shown on her face because Daisy blinked. However, before she could say something, Daisy added, "We did chat sometimes, during classes. But we never play after school or on the weekends."

Okay, now her anger turned more into worry. Since Lucy lived a few houses away, Daisy had been allowed to visit her friend since turning ten years old. Anything could've happened to Daisy if she'd gone wandering.

Dawn forced herself to ask calmly, "Then where did you go every time you said you were going to Lucy's house?"

Daisy shrugged one shoulder. "Well, I usually just went behind the shed in our garden and wrote letters to Freddie. If it rained, then I'd go to Mrs. Smythe's house next door and she'd give me tea and biscuits." She bit her lip and asked, "Are you cross with me?"

For a second, Dawn didn't answer. While she was a little upset at the fact Daisy had lied to her—she hated lying more than anything—it was more fear for what could've happened that she struggled to control.

Daisy was far too trusting. One slightly crooked stranger could've taken her little girl away from her for good.

Daisy added quietly, "I won't do it again, I promise."

The words snapped Dawn back to the current situation. Needing to feel the comfort of Daisy's touch, she took her daughter's hand and squeezed. She said slowly so as to keep her voice calm, "I don't like that you lied to me. But you did tell me the truth and I hope you'll honor your promise to not lie to me again." Daisy bobbed her head a few times, and Dawn continued, "I do wish you would've said something sooner, Daisy. Are other kids or teachers treating you differently, too?"

She shrugged as she swung her feet above the floor again. "Some of them have been meaner. But I didn't like most of them anyway. Those of us who went to the dragon camp became our own group of friends. I also have Freddie and Emily."

Oh, Daisy. Her daughter had suffered on her own and never shown it.

She really was growing up.

Not caring that Daisy was eleven and maybe thought she was too old for it, Dawn tugged Daisy off the chair and helped her into her lap. Once she wrapped Daisy in a hug and laid her head against her daughter's, she said, "You've worked so hard to help other people like the dragon-shifters, haven't you?"

"I try. The dragon-shifters have always been nice to me. And I don't know why people would be mean to them or want to hurt them. Especially when most people have never met them. It seems silly. We're not supposed to judge without knowing someone, right? That's what you always tell me."

Dawn stroked her daughter's hair, smiling at how Daisy threw her own words back at her. And in a strange way, it was something she needed to hear considering everything that could happen. "Some people are afraid of what's different. I suppose I was one of those, too. I guess I need to listen to my own advice, huh?"

"Well, did you change your mind after tonight? Bram is nice. So is Mr. MacLeod. And you had fun with Mr. Whitby, too, right?"

"I'll admit that I'm less afraid now than when we first arrived here."

"So what are you going to do, Mum?"

The all-important question—what would Dawn do?

She took a second to squeeze Daisy tighter against her and merely revel in how much she loved her daughter.

However, as Daisy tried to turn around, Dawn leaned back to meet her eyes and said, "I have one more question first, love. Has anyone on Stonefire ever been mean to you? Or tried to scare you away?"

Daisy shook her head. "No, although Freddie says there are some older kids who tease everyone. So if they tease me, it'd almost be like I'm part of Stonefire, too. So I actually hope they do tease me soon."

Dawn bit back a smile. Daisy knew so much about the dragon clan, to the point she even knew how to be accepted among the younger crowd.

As she played with her daughter's hair, Dawn took a second to review all she knew and be absolutely certain of what she was going to say next.

Daisy was having more trouble with the kids at the human school than with the dragons.

Lucy and her mother had all but abandoned Daisy for her connection to the dragons she loved so much.

Daisy and Dawn both wanted another child in the family.

And through her daughter's enthusiasm, Dawn was

fairly sure she could become more comfortable around the dragon-shifters.

Not to mention she didn't love her current job, and she could find another, like she'd done a few times before.

There was really only one option to take.

Daisy shifted her position in her lap, and Dawn finally spoke again. "I'm not going to say yes to everything just yet. However, Bram said the doctor here can make Mr. Whitby's dragon quiet for a few days so I can talk with him. After that, I'll make my final decision. But in the meantime, you'll have to stay with Emily's family, provided they say it's okay."

Daisy frowned. "I can't stay here, too?"

Dawn smiled at Daisy's devastation. "Not yet. You have school, and I need some time alone with Blake, er, Mr. Whitby."

Daisy turned a little more to look better into her eyes. "So after a few days, you'll be celebrating a new baby coming?"

Blood rushed to Dawn's cheeks. Just how much had Freddie told Daisy about the mate-claim frenzy? She would have to find out more herself and then educate Daisy so she wasn't completely in the dark. After all, her daughter was eleven and would be a woman soon enough.

Dawn cleared her throat before saying, "No. If I decide to accept his dragon, then it'll happen after that. But don't get your hopes up just yet, Daisy Mae. Your father left us, and I don't want to go through that again with someone else and make us both sad. So I need to be sure about Mr. Whitby, at least a little, before disappearing with him, as your friend put it."

"Oh, I don't think Mr. Whitby would leave us. He's nice and would probably only want to protect you. Kind of like how Freddie wants to protect me."

She finally smiled again at the absolute certainty in Daisy's voice. "We'll see, love. We'll see." She moved Daisy off her lap and stood. "Let's find Emily's mother first, and then I'll talk with Bram again. If Emily's mother says it's okay, promise me you'll be on your best behavior. No wandering off or telling lies, among other things."

Daisy hopped from foot to foot, a sign she was excited. "I promise, Mum. If there's even a small chance we can live on Stonefire, I'll be the most bestest behaved girl ever."

Dawn couldn't help but laugh at how Daisy was laying it on thick. "Too bad I won't be around to see that." She took Daisy's hand. "Come on then. There's still a lot to do."

As she led her daughter back out to the great hall, Dawn wondered how long it would be before she could see Blake again. Now that she'd made a decision, she was eager to get started. Only then could she truly know which pathway her life would end up taking.

But then Daisy began tugging her hand to hurry up, and she pushed all other thoughts away. First things first —she needed to entrust Daisy into Mariana Barlow's care. Then she could ask about Blake.

Chapter Six

Blake stared at the ceiling of his hospital room, unsettled with the complete silence and emptiness inside his mind. One he hadn't experienced since his dragon had first talked with him at age six, a little over thirty years ago.

He vaguely remembered Dr. Sid drugging his dragon silent but not much else until he'd woken up a few minutes ago.

Well, except for Dawn Chadwick. Even without his dragon demanding they find and fuck her, his thoughts were full of the human female.

Her smile, her easy teasing, the way she made him feel relaxed and not anxious like he was with most people.

For the first time, Blake admitted how much he wanted a chance with a female.

Not that it was going to happen. She'd be long gone by now, for sure. Humans who didn't know much about dragon-shifters were afraid of the frenzy and all that it entailed.

Not only that, but Dawn also had her daughter to think of. Like most humans, she probably thought she needed to protect her child from the dragons despite the fact dragon-shifters usually treasured their children more than many humans did.

Maybe he should've tried to explain things better to Dawn and not kept the true mate pull a secret. Perhaps she might've run anyway. But there was a chance she wouldn't have fled without talking to him more.

If his inner beast were awake, he'd probably mention how he'd been right and Blake had been wrong.

He missed his bloody annoying dragon.

A knock on the door brought him out of his head, and in the next second, Dr. Sid Jackson—Stonefire's head doctor—walked in wearing a lab coat and her hair in the usual ponytail. She stopped at his bedside and asked softly, "Is your dragon still silent?"

Sid was a brilliant doctor and usually didn't blink at barking orders or getting reluctant dragon-shifters in line. However, her dragon had been silent for twenty years as a result of receiving too many shots of the silent dragon drug Blake himself had received. That usually meant she was a bit gentler with patients she had to drug herself.

He replied, "Yes, he's quiet and absent from my mind."

Sid bobbed her head. "While I won't exactly say good, it's what we need for your next visitor."

He frowned. "Visitor? Who? Bram? I don't think any of my current projects need explaining to anyone else."

Sid studied him a beat before replying, "Dawn Chadwick is here to see you."

He blinked. "What?"

Sid raised her brows. "You don't want to see her then?"

"No, no, I didn't say that. I'm just surprised, is all."

Could it be that his fated female was stronger than he'd thought? Maybe he needed to not judge her so quickly.

Of course, maybe she just wanted to be polite and say no thanks. And also maybe to tell him to leave her and her daughter alone.

Either way, he wouldn't know unless he talked with her. Even without his dragon, his heart rate sped up a fraction at the thought of seeing the beautiful human again. If he were extremely lucky, she might even smile once for him.

The doctor studied him again before saying, "You shouldn't be surprised. I think she fancies you, Blake, and you know her daughter loves dragon-shifters almost more than anything. Although tell me straight—do you want to see her? Because if you're going to brush her off and pretend finding your true mate is no big deal, I'll spare her the drama."

Blake wasn't usually so forthright with people, but Sid had been there when his mother had become sick and had helped her to the very end. He didn't owe the doctor anything, but he respected her. So he replied, "I know it's a big deal. It's just that she flinched the first time she saw my flashing eyes a couple hours before the kiss happened. So I wasn't exactly sure what to think."

Sid grunted. "Well, she stood up to Bram so give her some credit. Just talk with her and see what happens. But don't string her along too much, Blake. She has her daughter to think of."

He raised his brows. "When did you start giving relationship advice?"

Sid shrugged. "I only reserve it for stubborn dragon-shifters who make up excuses as to why they shouldn't have a mate."

He opened his mouth but promptly closed it. The bloody doctor was too good.

Sid tilted her head. "So? Will you see her?"

Maybe before the kiss he could've pretended Dawn and her daughter were too much work. Or he could rationalize away about how they would take too much time away from his research.

Or come up with a million other excuses, really.

However, his dragon was now involved. And the last thing he wanted to do was to cause his inner beast unnecessary pain. Because that was exactly what would happen if Dawn fled and he didn't go through the frenzy—years of pain and struggle for them both.

Since she'd made the effort to see him, he at least needed to give Dawn a chance.

Blake said, "Show her in."

"I will. But Nikki will be just outside the door, listening for trouble. So be careful. You know what could happen if you touch her."

It might wake his inner dragon. And Nikki was one of Stonefire's Protectors in charge of clan security. More than that, she was the second-in-command and someone a person didn't want to piss off if they could help it.

In a way, he was glad for Nikki to be nearby. The last thing he wanted was to hurt Dawn, whether unintentionally or not.

Before he could say he wouldn't distress any female on purpose, Sid left and shut the door behind her.

And even though it was probably only a matter of seconds, it felt as if years passed before there was a tentative knock on the door.

He shouted, "Come in."

The door swung inward, revealing Dawn dressed in clothes that were too big for her small frame.

Not that he cared. His eyes were glued to her face, her bright eyes and full lips just as perfect as before.

She had to be the most bloody beautiful female he'd ever seen. How in the hell he'd managed to find her as his true mate, he had no idea.

"Hello," she said as she walked into the room and shut the door behind her.

Even though he knew they needed to keep a distance between them, he wished she would come closer. "Hello, Dawn."

Silence fell for a few beats, a painful contrast to the last time they'd met.

Of course now she had to be aware of what a mate-claim frenzy entailed and was probably afraid his dragon would wake up and try to claim her.

As he tried to think of how to calm her fears at least a little, she finally spoke again. "It's almost strange not to see your flashing pupils. I know it startled me at first, but

I've seen so many pairs over the last twelve or so hours that it's almost normal."

Her comment was yet another reminder that his dragon—and best friend—was silent. However, he didn't think she was intentionally trying to cause him pain. Instead, he focused on the rest of her words. "What have you been doing for the last twelve hours?"

She laughed, the sound a balm to his very center. Was it always this way with true mates, that they seemed to be too perfect for words? Yet another instance of how Blake's self-imposed isolation had kept him in the dark.

Dawn replied, "Let's just say that getting a dragon child to bed can be a bit tougher with both personalities fighting it. And before you ask, I'm staying with Sasha Atherton right now."

He smiled. "Well, Freddie and his brother are a bit more energetic than most. Good luck with that." He paused and decided small talk could wait. It was time to be blunt. "Why are you still here, Dawn? I thought you would've run."

She took a step closer and tilted her head. "Did you want me to run?"

He blurted, "No."

"Good. I know this is all a bit awkward, but I just wanted to talk with you again. I only have a few days to make a very important decision, and getting to know you better will help me to make it."

He wished his dragon was awake so his inner beast could get to know Dawn, too. But that was impossible, and so he decided to embrace what he could while he still had it. "So they told you about the mate-claim frenzy then and all it entails?"

She bobbed her head. "Yes, and I'm not fully against the idea. But I've been hurt badly before and want to try and make sure it won't happen again."

Her bastard ex. A growl escaped before he could check it. "I would never abandon our child. Whatever happens, even if we don't suit as mates for the long-term, I will always be involved in our child's life and do my best to protect him or her."

She searched his gaze. "And what about Daisy? Even if she's not yours, she will probably need protection, too, if we live here. There aren't many humans on Stonefire."

"There are more than you think. And our clan isn't like some in that we welcome humans now. If Melanie or Evie so much as got a word of mistreatment, there'd be bloody hell to pay."

Melanie had been a human sacrifice given to Stonefire a few years ago and had ultimately written a book about dragon-shifters, paving the way for better understanding. She and Evie unofficially oversaw all the humans on Stonefire, sometimes with help from another human named Jane.

Dawn replied, "While I'm glad for it, Daisy needs some sort of stability. I think it'd break her heart to have you dote on any child of ours but ignore her."

He blinked. "I never said I would ignore her. I'll be honest and say that it'll take time to care for her as I've only met her recently—much like you. But she will be the half sibling of any child of ours, if you go through the frenzy. And that equates family in my book."

Dawn searched his eyes again, and he hoped he'd said the right thing. He wasn't good with humor to ease a situation like some, or pretty words to impress.

He just said the truth. And often, people didn't like it.

She took another step closer. Maybe he should've told her to stay by the door, but it brought her close enough for her scent to reach his nose. And her feminine musk mixed with something lightly floral calmed him.

"Well, then I guess that means we should do a sort of speed dating to see if we suit?" She lifted her mobile in her hand and waved it back and forth. "I can even set a timer on my phone, if you like, to make it seem more real, complete with an annoying buzzer sound."

And just like that, her words lightened the mood.

Blake had never had someone really try to do that with him before. Well, unless they'd been after him to shift so they could touch his lucky spot.

However, Dawn didn't even know about the damn spot. She merely wanted to know him.

Which made him want her all the more.

He waved toward the chair against the wall. "It's probably best if you sit over there whilst we do it."

She grinned and sat in the chair. "Right, then are you ready? Sixty seconds each, to keep it short and sweet? You can even ask the first question."

He couldn't remember the last time he'd played any sort of game. Blake spent most of his time on work, or flying, or swimming in the lake.

And yet, he'd never wanted to do something more. "I think it's time to get started, but you can ask the first question since it was your idea."

"Okay." She pressed her phone to start the timer, and he waited to see what Dawn would ask him.

FOR THE FIRST minute or so after she'd entered Blake's room, Dawn hadn't been sure if she'd made the right decision. She knew Blake was shy and not the most social person in the world, but it had been tense and awkward.

However, he'd soon opened up and even said Daisy would be considered family if they went through the frenzy.

That had been one of her biggest worries. Sure, she still needed to ensure Blake confirmed his words with actions, but it was a start.

Which had led her to asking him to play her silly speed dating idea. And surprisingly, he'd agreed, making her think there were more layers to the dragonman than he let on.

So she pressed the button for the countdown timer and asked a light question first. "What's your favorite food?"

He scowled a little. "Is that what you really want to waste your question on?" She raised her brows, nodded, and he answered, "Any type of pasta. Can you cook pasta?"

"Somewhat. Although if all else fails, there's always the sauce jars." He scrunched his nose and she laughed. "Well, then you can do the cooking, if it comes to that."

He smiled. "I can cook fairly well, actually, so that's not a problem."

Just as she was about to ask more, the timer went off. Blake raised his brows and she reset it. She motioned toward him. "Okay, I'll start it as soon as you start talking."

He didn't hesitate. "What do you like to do for yourself? Not for Daisy or as a mother, but for yourself?"

Dawn had to think about that for a second. Her life had been consumed with her daughter—how to take care of her, earning enough to keep them in their home, and even acting as both mother and father to her—for years.

But sometimes, when she had a spare minute, Dawn did do a few things for herself. She answered, "I like to draw and occasionally paint."

"Draw what?"

She shrugged. "Flowers, mostly. And sometimes birds or other small animals. Maybe if I get the chance, I could try my hand at a dragon."

"I'd love to see something of yours, later, when there's not a bloody buzzer about to go off."

And right on cue, it did.

She chuckled. "I won't apologize for the buzzer. This is quite fun, more than I thought it would be. Now, my turn." She reset it again and decided to ask a slightly more serious question this time. Hopefully Blake wouldn't shut down. "Why do you live apart from everyone else? Sasha showed me where your cabin is, and it's just along the boundary of the clan's land."

He paused for a second, and she wondered if he'd refuse to answer

Apparently, Blake didn't reveal much to people,

according to Sasha. And her new friend had warned against asking about his dragon until they were more comfortable with each other.

Which, of course, had made Dawn all the more curious.

So asking about his remote home was the closest she could do right now.

He finally said, "I like privacy. I did try living closer to everyone else, but the attention distracted me from my work."

It was hard not to ask why—but she had a feeling it dealt with his dragon—so she asked instead, "What are you working on right now? You made it sound important last night."

"That is a very long answer. But the short version is that it's to help protect the clan from one of our enemies."

The bloody timer went off again before she could ask for more details. But Blake didn't so much as blink and pointed toward it, wanting his turn. With a sigh, she reset it, and he asked, "Tell me what your perfect day would be."

"Hmm, I'm not sure. I suppose sunny and warm, and somewhere either along a lake, the sea, or even a wide-open valley. Somewhere with few people and an abundance of nature. I live in Manchester proper, and you can't really find that in the city. A park isn't quite the same."

"I imagine not."

She studied him. "Have you never been to Manchester?"

He shook his head. "I've never been to a human city, ever. I've only visited a few villages in the Lake District, and that was back when I was a teenager."

Dawn wished she knew more about all the laws and rules concerning dragon-shifters. But at the risk of sounding stupid, she asked, "Because you can't?"

He shrugged. "I could visit them sometimes, provided I follow all the laws. However, I hate large crowds. And the smells are overwhelming, not to mention all the noise. Some dragon-shifters like it, or at least tolerate it, but both my beast and I can't stand it. It's hard enough to do so in a village or a human restaurant so a proper city is out of the question."

She was about to ask if it was more to do with how the humans viewed him since he was a dragon-shifter. Even if he covered up the tattoo on his bicep, his usual flashing pupils would still give him away. However, the timer beeped again. She muttered, "This is really starting to irritate me. Just when we get to the good bits, it goes off."

Blake chuckled, and the sound made her smile. It was deep and soothing, and something she'd like to hear more often.

Pushing aside that realization, she asked, "What?"

He grinned. "You're cute when you're irritated."

She almost smiled at that. "Just don't be on the receiving end or you may change your story. I don't anger often, but when I do, I tend to lose most of my head and shout like a bloody banshee."

He shook his head. "You're on dragon land now, Dawn. It takes more than shouting to scare any of us."

She grunted. "We'll see. I'm sure someone will put that to the test some day."

He raised an eyebrow. "And it'll just show that I'm right."

As they stared at one another, exchanging smiles, Dawn had a realization—she wouldn't say no to Blake and the frenzy.

However, she was having too much fun with him to give her answer just yet. She could have at least a little more time before she committed and set things in motion. Maybe she could ask Sasha or even Evie some more questions to better prepare herself.

A knock was followed by a blond-haired male doctor entering the room. She didn't know his name, but he spoke with a Scottish accent. "We haven't officially met, but I'm Dr. Gregor Innes. And I'm afraid visiting time is over for now. Cassidy said you can come back later, Dawn, and have dinner with Blake if you like. But we need to do an examination and a few tests in the meantime."

Dawn stood. "Okay." She looked at Blake again. "I'll have another game for us to play when I visit later, so make sure you're ready."

The corner of his mouth ticked up, the slight change making him even more handsome to Dawn. Not that it was hard to do. His hazel eyes and slightly disheveled hair made her want to go over, smooth the wild locks, and touch the stubble on his cheeks just to feel the raspiness against her fingers.

Maybe even place a hand on his chest and see if he

had the same toned muscles as the other dragon-shifters she'd seen so far.

She also recalled his scent from the day before, when they'd been working in close quarters. An earthy mixture of man, woods, and something she couldn't define.

It was official—it really had been too long since she'd been with a man.

Blake answered and brought her back to the present, "I look forward to it."

Before she could get lost in another daydream about Blake and what he hid under his clothes, Dawn waved goodbye.

And she couldn't stop smiling as she met up with the dragonwoman named Nikki and headed out of the surgery. It'd been so long since she'd dated and she'd feared it would be boring, awkward, or both. However, she had actually enjoyed herself.

Maybe, just maybe, Blake was her second chance.

Chapter Seven

Hours later, Dawn did her best not to swing the tote bag in her hand. Her daughter wasn't the only one who became fidgety when they were anxious—Dawn did, too. She wasn't so much nervous as eager to start her almost second date with Blake.

Mostly because she might have to start the frenzy the next day, to be on the safe side, and she wanted to spend as much time with him as she could before the massive life-changing event.

Walking at her side was the dark-haired form of Sasha Atherton. She'd volunteered to escort Dawn to the surgery so that Nikki could spend some time with her young daughter. Sasha wasn't a Protector, but her brother Zain was. And a rather good one that no one wanted to mess with, meaning they should be safe enough for a short walk.

The dragonwoman spoke up. "This isn't a race, you

know. Blake will still be there if we walk at a normal pace."

Dawn didn't realize she'd been power walking and slowed her speed to normal. "Sorry, but it's been so long since I've been eager to see a man for a date, let alone have a night free without worrying about Daisy. I'm just excited, I guess."

She'd talked to her daughter about forty-five minutes ago. Daisy had been her usual, cheerful self, and seemed to be enjoying her time with Emily's family.

Dawn still missed her, though. It had been just her and Daisy for so long that it was strange to spend any length of time away from her.

But it couldn't be helped, not if she was to ensure Daisy could keep up her relationship with Freddie and the other dragon children. So Dawn focused back on Sasha and said, "I thought dragon-shifters were in great shape. Are you saying that a mere human wears you out?"

Sasha snorted. "Look at you, being all sassy. I like you more and more, Dawn. I'm glad you're going to live on Stonefire, and not just because it means Freddie won't ask me constantly about when he can see Daisy again."

"They are quite attached, aren't they?"

Sasha nodded. "Yes, but it's good for the both of them, I think. At least in Freddie's case, his behavior has improved a bit these days. He was never a troublemaker, but his mind can wander sometimes in school. He's much better now, almost as if he needs to learn every little thing so he can help Daisy understand it, too. He might even become a model student so he can help her when she starts school here."

"Just maybe don't sit them next to each other in class or nothing will get done."

Sasha smiled. "That will be up to the teachers. If they don't realize that now, they'll learn it soon enough." Sasha threaded her arm through Dawn's and added, "I'm glad you're here, too. And not just for me and my boy, either. You and Blake are both lonely people, and I'm beyond thrilled that you two have a chance now."

Maybe with anyone else Dawn would deny it. However, Sasha had become a good friend in such a short amount of time. She was the first true female friend Dawn had made in years, maybe ever since her ex-husband had left her. "Nothing is guaranteed, Sasha, and you know it."

The dragonwoman shrugged one shoulder. "Maybe. But if two good-hearted people can't make a true-mate pairing work, then I don't know who can. Especially since me and my mate—who I didn't much care for as a child but ended up becoming my perfect match later on— made it and still act lovey-dovey at times, as my boys can attest to with semi-disgusted frowns."

Dawn chuckled. "That's part of your job, though, to annoy your children at times."

Sasha winked. "Of course it is. It wouldn't be fun otherwise."

The outline of the surgery came into view, and Dawn reluctantly changed the subject, reminding herself that she should have lots more time to talk with Sasha if everything went well with Blake. "My second—and last date before I have sex with him—is about to start. It's weird to think of it in those terms."

Sasha met her gaze, amusement twinkling in them. "Oh, it's more than mere sex, my friend. A mate-claim frenzy is an experience unlike any other."

Even though she had asked Sasha a few questions about how the frenzy worked, Dawn had held back asking about her fears. Seeing as she would be going through with one soon enough, she decided to be bold and finally ask, "It's not scary, is it?"

Her friend raised her brows. "I can't imagine a mate-claim frenzy with Blake ever being scary. And no, I'm not insulting the male. He's just reserved, and kind, and the type of male to place a spider outside rather than kill it." Sasha cleared her throat. "That doesn't really sound the best. It won't be boring, though. His dragon half will make sure of that. Usually, the inner beast takes control for the second round before they almost tag team between them." Sasha leaned closer and whispered, "And who knows, sometimes the quiet ones can surprise you."

Dawn's cheeks heated at the thought of Blake naked and above her, growling as he thrust and claimed her. She wouldn't mind a little surprise in that department. Especially since her last long-term sexual relationship had been with her ex, and that had involved a lot of timetables and charts to try to conceive. Even before switching to IVF methods, the initial spark had vanished.

Which only reminded her that it'd been a long time since she'd had sex and she only hoped she didn't disappoint him.

No. It would be fine. Well, hopefully more than fine. She'd find out soon enough.

They reached the surgery and went inside. However, they stopped in the reception area and Sasha motioned toward the front desk. "Go and have a good time, Dawn. You deserve it. Just call me when you're done and I'll take you back."

She bobbed her head and they said their goodbyes, complete with Sasha winking at her.

The more she interacted with the clan members of Stonefire, the more she liked them. Maybe one day she could truly fit in. Dawn didn't worry about Daisy—her daughter would force her way into everyone's hearts within a few months—but Dawn hoped she could do it, too. After so many years of being a single mum, she'd almost forgotten what it was like to do more than work and take care of Daisy.

But all of that didn't matter this evening. So she pushed aside her doubts and chatted with the man at reception before being led into the back area, where Blake was staying.

It was time to make the most of her second—and final—date with the man she would soon be having a child with.

BLAKE HAD TALKED to more people in the last few hours than he usually did in a month.

It seemed everyone had advice or warnings to give him.

Although Bram's visit was the one that lingered. He'd told Blake that Dawn needed to give her definitive answer tonight about the frenzy. Even though technically his dragon should stay silent for nearly two more days, none of the doctors or Bram wanted to risk it. If Blake's dragon woke up early, he might go after Dawn before she was ready.

And then any chance they might've had would probably vanish.

Although how he was supposed to win her over, as Bram put it, Blake had no bloody idea. It was one thing to tease and play a game, but quite another to ask, "Are you ready to start a sex marathon with me?"

His dragon would probably have some suggestions, but the deafening silence inside his mind only reinforced how that wasn't an option.

A knock was immediately followed by Dawn entering his room. The mere sight of the human female drove away his worries, which he didn't fully understand. Just because someone was your true mate didn't mean they had magic over you.

But for all he knew, that's how it worked. Blake had never had a lasting relationship with any female. Every attempt had ended in disaster because of their obsession with his damn spot in dragon form, which meant it was all new to him.

Regardless, Dawn seemed to have better fitting clothes now—maybe hers had arrived—and she carried a large, bulky tote bag in one hand. Not wanting an awkward silence, he decided to start the conversation for a change. "What mayhem do you have planned for this evening?"

She grinned. "Mayhem is a word you don't hear enough. I like it. Although now it sets me up for something much grander than what I have planned."

After shutting the door, Dawn pulled a chair toward him but stopped several feet away still. He asked, "Will we start before dinner?"

"Ah, but you see my game is part dinner, part entertainment."

His curiosity piqued, he adjusted his position on the bed and leaned forward a little. "Are you going to tell me or do I have to guess?"

"I don't think you'd be able to guess, if I'm honest. So it's best to just get started, right?"

Dawn reached out for the little side table on wheels that could be moved over his bed and maneuvered it in front of her. He watched as she took out several containers—all opaque, meaning he couldn't bloody see the contents—and then tossed the tote bag to the side.

Since he couldn't even smell the contents, a dragon-shifter must've helped her prepare it with all the special containers they used. Otherwise, all of the scents from the human-made ones would drive a dragon-shifter mad rather quickly.

Dawn tapped each of the lids as she talked. "I have a bunch of different dishes here, but everything's been colored with food dye. I want to see if you can guess what they are. And once you're done tasting, we can even come up with some new names for the oddly colored food."

He raised an eyebrow. "Couldn't I just guess by looking at them?"

"Ah, but here's the thing—you won't be able to see them for the first part. Maybe smell them—I can't help it, although I have some things to try to hide the scents—but Sasha did give me a blindfold to use." She tossed it at him and Blake caught it. "So, are you ready?"

He blinked as he stared at the blindfold. The activity was almost…childish.

Although he was more concerned with what the food would taste like, given what Dawn had told him earlier about her cooking skills. He didn't want to spit out something awful and hurt her feelings. So he blurted, "Did you cook everything?"

She tilted her head. "Clever man, remembering that I don't always cook well. Sasha helped me, so everything's edible. I'm going to eat some after the fact, too. It'll be our dinner."

Just the thought of Dawn working hard to make a variety of dishes to entertain him did something to Blake's heart. Maybe it was a childish game, but he didn't care. It was almost as if he wanted to be a little less serious when Dawn was around.

He waved the blindfold in the air. "What about you? This seems like a rather one-sided game, if you ask me."

She shrugged. "Oh, watching you try to feed yourself with a blindfold will be quite entertaining for me."

He raised his brows. "Maybe you should try it after me. That way it's fair—we both do something embarrassing."

She shook her head. "I know what all the dishes are, so it's not much of a guess."

He smirked. "I have some hospital snacks you can try."

Which were bland and almost tasteless.

She waved a hand in dismissal. "Fine, fine, I'll try something later, if you want. But you get to go first." She slapped her hands together and rubbed them. "Shall we get started?"

It was strange watching someone get so excited over something so minor. Blake was hard on himself and rarely celebrated his discoveries. However, there was something fascinating about how open Dawn was about everything. He could definitely get used to it.

Maybe even more than that—he could see himself becoming addicted to Dawn and all her quirks.

But that was still the future and he needed to focus on the present. It was time to try some of Dawn's food.

Blake lifted the blindfold almost to his face. "Promise me that you're not going to take any pictures or video of me doing this."

She snapped her fingers. "There went my plan to blackmail you."

The tone of her voice told him she was joking.

And Blake wasn't entirely sure how to tease back. Although he sensed that he would have to learn how to do that easier in the future since he could already tell that his true mate loved teasing and being playful.

For her, he would try not to hold back so much.

Blake twirled the blindfold—loving the sound of Dawn's laughter—and then placed it across his eyes. He could just imagine his dragon snorting while also encouraging the behavior. Out of the pair of them, Blake's dragon was the more easygoing half.

Once the material was tied in place, he cleared his throat. "I'm ready."

The first smelled to hit him was a strong scent of lavender, which was far too overpowering to be added to any dish. Which meant Dawn had probably brought along some lavender oil to mask the scent of the food.

She hadn't been kidding when she'd said she would try to disguise the smells. He didn't know if she'd just been thorough or if she'd received a lot of suggestions from Sasha Atherton.

Blake could hear her opening containers and finally wheeling the tray table toward him, the lavender smell growing even stronger. She said, "I know I'm not supposed to touch you, but I need to hand you the spoon. Can you handle that?"

The craving to feel even the slightest brush of her skin against his surged through his body. Even if his dragon woke up and he had to bloody fight off his beast, Blake didn't care. "Yes."

"Okay, here goes."

A spoon was pressed against his hand, and he waited for it…yes…the slightest brush of her fingers. It wasn't more than a whisper of heat and softness, but it was one of the most erotic caresses he'd ever experienced, thanks to the blindfold.

Maybe he needed to keep the scrap of material and use it on Dawn later, after the frenzy was over.

Yes, he was starting to think of much more than just the frenzy now.

All too soon, the touch vanished, and he did his best not to pout at the loss. He was a grown male, for crying out loud.

Dawn's voice filled the room. "Feel the edge of the little table thing and move slowly toward the first container."

As he followed her directions, he willed the food to not be terrible. Maybe with time, it would be easier to disappoint Dawn. However, in the here and now, he didn't want to upset her.

His usual penchant for honesty was being tested.

Regardless, he found the first container, clumsily tried to scoop some food and moved it toward his mouth.

DAWN KNEW the food-tasting and food coloring was immature. And yet, it was the perfect way to have some fun and not worry too much about awkward silences since Blake would focus on the food, and then they could talk about it afterward.

It also gave her a chance to study Blake for a bit.

With his eyes covered by the dark material, his face looked a little more rugged. And not just because of the stubble on his cheeks.

It took her a second to figure out what it was, and then it hit her—his eyes were almost always wary, as if someone was going to ask him something uncomfortable.

Probably something to do with his dragon.

Gah, Dawn wanted to see him shift so badly, knowing full well it might scare her a little at first. And yet she knew that couldn't happen until after the frenzy since Sasha had explained that a dragon-shifter needed to embrace their inner beast to change forms. And that was impossible with a dragon roaring to claim their true mate.

As Blake lifted the first spoonful of a dark purple concoction to his mouth, she pushed all other thoughts away and focused on the piece of cutlery at his lips.

Lips that were firm and yet soft, she remembered. Their accidental kiss seemed a million years ago already.

He finally swallowed the food and thankfully didn't blanch. Sasha had helped her make everything, but there was still always the chance she'd put in too much salt or cooked it too long. "Well?"

He tilted his head, the light highlighting his short hair. Not too short—she could still run her fingers through it—but not overly long, either.

She was a bit of a fool, really, studying a blasted man's hair. That must be what happened to a woman who hadn't gone on more than a few dates in over a decade.

Blake finally spoke. "I want to say tomato soup, but a sort of spicy variety."

She smiled. "Ding-ding, you're correct! I've never made it from scratch before, and it's a little lumpy, but you're still right. I can't wait for you to see what color I made it."

He raised his eyebrows. "Can I take this blindfold off now?"

"Try at least one more, and then we'll see. It's kind of fun watching you fumble about."

He muttered, "So much for my bloody PhD."

And for a second, Dawn wondered if she'd planned this all wrong. She'd never gone to university because she'd married young and had spent so many years trying to conceive a child. Did someone like Blake need higher-minded activities?

However, before doubt could set in, he smiled and added, "Just know that turnabout is fair play. Your turn with the blindfold will come one day, Dawn. So wait for it."

Her doubts faded at Blake's smile. She was definitely worrying too much. "Noted. Now, stop stalling. The food is getting cold, and if any of it is only so-so now, it'll be even worse cold."

Snorting, he felt around to the next container. "Even us dragon-shifters have these fancy things called microwaves."

Even though he couldn't see it, she stuck her tongue out. "Just hurry up and eat, dragonman. I want some, too."

He scooped a black-colored sauce—Dawn's experiment to get blue had failed—and watch him eat again. When he nodded afterward, her heart sung a little.

Blake said, "This one is great, some kind of pasta sauce. Although adding pasta itself to the mix would make it better."

She eyed the last container, which contained green spaghetti noodles. "I did bring some pasta, too. Take off your blindfold, and let's eat because I think the noodles might be congealing."

He chuckled, the sound echoing in the small room. Blake tore off the blindfold and zeroed in on the dishes in front of him. He prodded said noodles with his spoon. "These might be inedible."

Her stomach rumbled. "At this point, I don't care."

Blake met her gaze, and she forgot all about her hunger. Or, at least the kind related to her stomach.

The dragonman was too handsome for his own good.

The usual wariness in his eyes was gone, replaced with concern. He stated, "Then come and eat. No female of mine should ever be hungry."

While she wasn't technically his yet, Dawn didn't feel the need to correct him.

No, after her silly second-date antics and Blake putting up with them in good fun, she knew more than ever she wanted a chance with him.

Maybe if she were more methodical, Dawn would've pondered that thought some more, let it sit, and merely enjoy the rest of the evening without any heaviness or complications.

Or, she would've talked to Blake about what so many people had told her, that frenzies always worked between true mates regardless of fertility issues with others.

However, much like her daughter, Dawn's mouth and brain didn't always work together. So she blurted, "I want the frenzy, Blake. Do you?"

Chapter Eight

Blake wanted to shout yes, he wanted the frenzy before pulling Dawn close and kissing her. However, he couldn't do that just yet. A few things had to be set up quickly before any of that happened. So he simply stated, "Of course I do."

"You say 'of course' as if it couldn't be any other way."

He reached out a hand but then pulled back and clenched his fingers into a fist. "You are beautiful, kind, amusing, and so many other things. What male wouldn't want a chance with a female like that?"

Her cheeks turned pink, and he itched to caress her blush to see if her skin was warmer to the touch.

The whole "not being able to touch her" deal was annoying.

Dawn cleared her throat. "Maybe if said female were single without any strings attached. However, I have

Daisy, and not every bloke would be up for that challenge."

He frowned. "Maybe she's energetic and chatty, but so are you. If they like you, why wouldn't they like your daughter?"

Dawn tilted her head. "Liking her and wanting to raise her are two very different things."

Even now, he could tell her idiotic ex was hovering over her. He'd left because Daisy had been too much for him to handle, true. But the male must've hurt her deeper than she let most people see.

It was a good thing the bastard lived in Australia or Blake would risk venturing into a city to find him and tell him a few things. "She is a huge part of your life, a huge part of you. Maybe I would've resisted a little without knowing you, but now? I would accept five Daisies for a chance with you, Dawn. You make the world brighter, which is something I never thought I'd say to another person."

She moved a few inches closer, although it was still too bloody far away. Her voice was soft when she replied, "You're so much more than what people say about you, Blake. Why do you hide away from everyone else?"

He could've deflected like he usually did when people asked him about his self-imposed solitude. However, unlike with others, Dawn asking him didn't turn Blake defensive or make him want to ignore the whole matter. No, if she was willing to endure his dragon during the frenzy, then she deserved an answer. "White dragons are rare, but a white dragon with any other sort of special marking is almost unheard of. They're called unicorn dragons, and stories say that if you ever can find one, that you should ask to see their unique marking, touch it, and make a wish. It'll bring good luck and maybe even your greatest desire to life."

Blake did his best not to remember a lifetime of people trying to corner him somewhere so they could convince him to shift, touch his spot, and make a wish.

She whispered, "You're a unicorn dragon, aren't you?"

He nodded. "As a child, the other kids made fun of me constantly after my first shift in class. Children are so curious about what their dragon will be like, look like, and act like that it makes them a little insecure. Anything out of the ordinary is pounced upon to make themselves feel better.

"I didn't understand that as a child, of course, and just tried to hide away from everyone when I could. And to be honest, it became much worse as I grew up. Adults won't try to accost a child, but you'd be amazed at what someone will do to an adult unicorn dragon to get a chance at making a wish."

Dawn moved even closer while remaining about a foot away. There was a mixture of anger and sadness in her gaze. "What exactly did they do to you?"

He shrugged. "Nothing criminal, mind you. But pretty much my whole adult life dragon-shifters have tried a variety of ways to get me to shift. To say I gave up on dating or finding a mate was an understatement. No one could get past my dragon form, so I isolated myself and devoted myself to my work."

"That's horrible."

He searched her gaze. "Yes. Although you had no idea about anything related to my dragon form and you still found ways to make me smile the night of the play. And I somehow don't think the strangely colored food activity was a ploy to get me to shift, either."

She laughed. "No, that would've required some better-tasting food, for sure." Dawn moved the table away but didn't quite close the distance between them. She added, "I do want to see your dragon some day, but that's just because he's part of you. You could be bright pink and I wouldn't care, although I'm sure Daisy would love that."

His lips twitched. "I've never heard of a pink dragon, and to be honest, I'm not sure I'd want to be one. But a pink dragon wouldn't be a unicorn. It'd be more like another mythical creature. Say, a Pegasus."

"I hope another dragon color, like rainbow, doesn't show up because there aren't any more horse-like mythical creatures I can think of off the top of my head."

He full-on grinned. "Don't mention that to the Scottish dragon clan. The kelpie is quite famous up there, even if they are malevolent."

The kelpie was a mythical Scottish creature that often appeared in the form of a horse near streams and rivers. The outcome was usually in the kelpie's favor and bad for the humans who fell under their spell.

She chuckled. "I forgot about them. And I've even seen those two giant horse head sculptures called *The Kelpies* on the drive between Edinburgh and Stirling once. Maybe I need to see just how many different kind of horse-like mythical creatures there are. You know, to keep a list handy in case we need some more names."

He snorted—Blake couldn't remember the last time he'd done it so often in a conversation—and wondered what strange names the human would bestow on any dragon with even one tiny speck of another color in their hides.

And just like that, Dawn had relaxed him and made him smile despite sharing how strange his life had been as a white dragon with a black spot.

He'd been skeptical of true mates for a long time, but Blake was starting to think fate had been right in his case.

Sobering, Blake decided they needed to get back on topic. "That's a fun project you could do with Daisy. However, let's circle back to the part where you said you wanted to go through the frenzy with me. Are you absolutely certain?"

Dawn bobbed her head. "Yes. I went through all the reasons in my head earlier about what it would mean for Daisy, for me, and our lives in general. Daisy wants to live on Stonefire, and I'm far more open to it now. And spending more time with you hasn't scared me away or made me want to flee but rather quite the opposite. So what needs to be done to get the frenzy started?"

Maybe some would laugh at Dawn's naïveté regarding her question, but not Blake. It showed him that she made goals and saw them through. What male wouldn't respect that?

He motioned toward the mobile phone on the small stand next to his bed. "I'll need to call Bram and have a cottage set up for us. Mine is too remote, and we need to be closer to everyone for your sake."

She searched his gaze. "What do you mean for my sake?"

He shrugged. "Some humans scare easily when the dragon half comes out. And if you want to leave, others will need to ensure you can. Whilst my human half will fight to let you go, my dragon may not be so easily tamed."

"Oh."

He laid his hand an inch from Dawn's on the bed, loving how he could feel the heat of her skin even if they weren't touching. "I hope you won't run, though. I like you, Dawn. And it'd be nice to date you some more."

She smiled, vanquishing any anxiety that had been lingering on her face. "Maybe some would think it strange, but I did it all the right way before—dating, engagement, wedding, child—and it didn't work out. Perhaps I need to do it out of order. It'll certainly make things interesting."

Blake barely resisted closing the distance between them and kissing her.

He needed to call Bram ASAP and get everything in motion so he could do that, and more, to his beautiful human. "Then quickly eat a little of what you brought before getting something warm at the clan's restaurant. I'll call Bram and take care of everything."

She picked up the spoon and prodded the cold noodles. "Maybe I should risk the bland hospital snacks instead."

With a chuckle, he handed over what he had and

simply enjoyed watching Dawn eat. She was so free with her emotions, making a face at the plain rice cakes and then moaning at the small piece of chocolate one of the Protectors had smuggled in for him.

Blake couldn't wait to see what other responses he could get from her.

The frenzy couldn't start soon enough.

Chapter Nine

Two mornings later, Dawn couldn't help but pick at the hem of her top as she waited in front of a stone cottage, the Protector named Nikki at her side.

She hadn't slept much the last two nights. No, her mind had run a million miles a minute with various scenarios of how a frenzy would play out.

Ever since Dawn had said yes, she'd been kept apart from Blake to allow his inner dragon to return. And even though they'd only met recently, she'd had a hard time staying away or not calling him.

Apparently, all the years she'd told herself that she didn't need a partner in life, how she could handle Daisy on her own and be perfectly content, had been a lie. Yes, Dawn could—and had proven—she could take care of her daughter on her own. But spending time with Blake, and even Sasha, had revealed how truly lonely she'd been.

Nikki's voice cut through her thoughts. "Do you still want to do this?"

She nodded and met the dragonwoman's brown-eyed gaze. "Of course. The waiting has been nerve-wracking, is all."

"Well, take it from someone who had the frenzy all of a sudden with a male who acted as if he didn't even like her, and I can tell you that being prepared is much better."

She'd met Nikki's mate, Rafe, only briefly. But he'd smiled and been nice enough to Dawn. "It's obvious he loves you now, regardless of what happened."

Nikki raised an eyebrow. "You're one very perceptive human, Dawn."

She shrugged. "Wait until your daughter is older. Then you'll learn that a parent has to be perceptive, especially if their kid likes to explore new things or go wandering."

Nikki sighed. "I'm sure Louisa will be a handful given who her father is. But for now, she's easy enough to keep track of." Nikki searched her gaze a second before adding, "So, are you ready?"

Taking a deep breath, Dawn bobbed her head. "Yes."

"Good. Remember to call if anything is too much or you get frightened. One of us Protectors will be stationed nearby, at a discreet enough distance to allow you a bit of privacy, awaiting any calls. Now, follow me."

They entered the cottage and went upstairs. Nikki stopped in front of a door and knocked. At Blake's muffled "Come in," Nikki opened the door.

Dawn instantly found Blake's gaze. His pupils flashed quickly, telling her his dragon was back.

But while she was still a little unsure of how everything would play out, it didn't scare her anymore. If anything, she was curious about getting to know his second half better.

Blake murmured, "You came."

She sighed. "Why does everyone keep acting surprised that I'm here today? If I can raise and take care of my daughter on my own for nearly a decade, then I can handle one man's dragon."

Blake's pupils flashed again. "I hope so."

Nikki moved to the doorway. "Have fun, you two. And Blake, don't do anything I wouldn't do."

With a wink, the dragonwoman shut the door, leaving Dawn alone with Blake.

He motioned for her to come forward. "It's taking everything I have to control my dragon right now. But I'll hold him back as long as you need. Come to me when you're ready, Dawn."

Eager for the next phase of her life to begin, she crossed the distance and stood a few inches away from him. Looking up, she murmured, "I think it's time for you to kiss me again, dragonman."

And she waited to see if he would.

BOTH MAN and beast had scented Dawn the instant she had entered the house.

She'd come after all.

His dragon growled. *Of course she did. She's our true mate. Why wouldn't she?*

Saying yes and then having two days to think about it? It's possible she could've changed her mind.

Well, she didn't. She's here, and she's ours. Don't waste too much time talking or I'll take control.

Before he could reply, Nikki and Dawn walked into his room.

He met Dawn's gaze and his dragon hummed. *She's here, and so close. I want to touch her, kiss her, fuck her. Now.*

He barely noticed the short exchange he had with his human, replying on autopilot since he needed to keep his dragon in check.

Then his female finally walked up to him and murmured, "I think it's time for you to kiss me again, dragonman."

Not needing any coaxing from his dragon, he reached out and pulled her up against his body. Despite the layers of clothing between them, heat surged and his cock turned to stone.

His beast said, *Kiss her. Now. She's here and waiting. She's more than ready for us.*

Somehow resisting the sweet scent of her arousal, Blake raised a hand and cupped her cheek. He said to his dragon, *Give me a minute or two. She's human, and I don't want to scare her.*

Fine. But not more than a few minutes. I want her.

As he stroked the soft skin of her cheek, he whispered, "You're so lovely, Dawn. It's hard to believe you're mine now."

The corner of her mouth ticked up. "Yours for the

frenzy, but we'll see how it goes after. Remember, you haven't lived with Daisy full-time yet."

"It'll take more than a child to scare away a dragonman."

Before she could reply, he lowered his head until he was a hairbreadth from her mouth. Her breathing quickened against his lips, and he asked, "Are you ready?"

Her reply was to close the distance between their faces, pressing her lips to his.

At the contact, a driving need once again coursed through his body, like it had the night of the play. He wanted to hold her, kiss her, and fuck her until she carried his scent and their child.

His dragon hummed. *Yes, yes, rip off her clothes and fuck her. Now. She is ours to claim. We need to make sure no one else tries to take her away.*

Blake managed to push his dragon's need to the side for a few seconds, sliding his tongue into her mouth. He groaned as he slowly explored it, stroking her tongue with his, loving how she tasted.

A male could get lost in her mouth alone.

His dragon roared. *No, no, no, her mouth isn't enough. I want her naked, and under us, and our cock inside her.*

As Dawn threaded her fingers through his hair and kissed him back, matching him stroke for stroke, he moaned and pulled her even tighter against him.

The feel of her hard nipples against his chest made his dragon stand up and roar. Not wanting to lose his chance, Blake broke the kiss and asked, "Are you attached to these clothes?"

"Not really."

"Good." Extending a talon, he sliced the back of her top and then her skirt. As the pieces gaped open, he ran a hand against her bare skin and kissed her neck. "So soft and warm." He arched away from her to let the skirt fall to the floor.

Afraid he wouldn't be able to stop his beast from flipping her over and fucking her from behind if he saw her in nothing but her underwear, he took her lips again. He licked, stroked, and desperately tried to let Dawn know how she drove him crazy.

He'd never tasted anything so perfect in his life. Crazy as it was, he didn't think he'd ever tire of his human.

His dragon growled. *Stop stalling. Shred her panties and fuck her. She needs to be claimed. She's ours. No other male should have her.*

He finally broke the kiss and stepped away slightly. Before Dawn could ask anything, he flicked a talon to remove the scraps of her underwear as her top fell to the floor. His mouth watered at her small breasts encased in lace. Unable to resist, he leaned over and took a tight bud between his lips and suckled.

Dawn groaned and arched her back.

His dragon grunted. *No, no. She needs to be naked. You can suck her nipples later. I need to be inside her. She needs to carry our young.*

As he released her, he cut through the side of her bra and slid it off her shoulders.

And for a second, they stared at one another. He was fully clothed, and she naked, but he couldn't tear his gaze from her slightly swollen lips or flushed cheeks.

Then she smiled and said, "Take off your clothes, Blake. It's my turn to touch you, too."

Without hesitation, he stepped back and ripped off his clothes.

As soon as he moved closer to her again, she reached out a hand and lightly caressed his chest, rubbing back and forth in his small patch of light brown hair. She murmured, "You're so strong."

Taking her hand, he kissed her palm and then yanked her against him, loving how she sucked in a breath when their skin touched. Her soft belly against his cock nearly made him come right then and there.

His beast said, *Do you want to waste your chance that way? Because our deal was the first orgasm was yours, then it's my turn.*

Knowing his dragon was serious, Blake placed a possessive hand on Dawn's soft arse and murmured, "You can admire me at length later, love. But you can feel how much I want you. Do you really want to talk right now?"

She snorted. "I could if I put my mind to it."

He moved his hand down from her arse to between her legs, loving how wet and swollen she was. Dawn gasped and he asked, "But do you really want to?"

Digging her nails into his back, she shook her head. "No."

"Good."

He took her lips in a hard, crushing kiss as he gently stroked her center.

His beast hissed. *She's so hot and wet. Toss her on the bed, spread her legs, and fuck her already.*

Blake decided to stop fighting his beast. And so as he continued kissing her, he moved them toward the bed.

When they were close enough, he broke the kiss and gently laid her down.

He took a second to take in her body, loving every curve and even the stretch marks on her belly. She was a female who had lived life a little, which made her all the more perfect for him.

His beast hissed. *Hurry up. Your turn is almost over, and I'm not going to remind you again.*

His dragon's words snapped him back to the present and the fact he was about to start a mate-claim frenzy with the human lying on his bed.

Wanting to enjoy her while he was still in control, Blake covered her body with his. He reached down and stroked her pussy slowly, attune to every movement she made as he did it. He murmured, "Let's make sure you're nice and ready. Because once my dragon takes over, it's going to be hard and fast, love."

And so he entered a finger inside her and watched her face as she squirmed.

Much like during their two "dates," she displayed her emotions freely. He couldn't wait to see what others he could get out of his female, too.

Dawn had been kissed many times in her life, but nothing compared to how Blake devoured her mouth as if he could never get enough.

She barely blinked when he shredded her clothes—it actually sent a tiny thrill through her body—and soon enough, she was on a bed with the dragonman on top of her.

And his wicked fingers made her forget about anything but how close she already was to coming.

Then his fingers were gone and he murmured, "You're more than ready, I think." She felt the head of his cock at her entrance. "You're about to become mine, Dawn. All mine."

She threaded her fingers into his hair and moved his head until she could see his eyes. His pupils flashed a few times before remaining round. However, the hunger in his gaze—like he would die if he didn't have her—made her heart skip a beat.

No man had ever looked at her like that, not even her ex.

No. Right here, right now, it was all about Blake and only him. The rest of her life would return soon enough.

She arched her back, loving how his cock slid against her. "Then fuck me, dragonman. I'm ready."

If her words surprised him, he didn't show it. Instead, he kissed her as he slowly entered her.

She'd barely gotten a glance at his cock, but she groaned as he stretched her in a good way.

He broke the kiss and swore. "You're so bloody tight, Dawn."

Not wanting to reflect on just how long it'd been since she'd had sex, she lightly scratched his back and moved downward until she could grab one of his firm arse cheeks. "Don't stop, Blake. Don't you dare stop."

With a growl, he plunged the rest of the way inside

her, and Dawn moaned. Then his finger brushed her clit, and all rational thought left her head.

As he moved his hips and swirled her tight bud, Dawn wanted to feel his mouth on hers and yanked his head down. She didn't care that their teeth clashed lightly. She licked and tasted, moving in time to Blake's thrusts.

Damn, she'd missed sex, and kissing, and merely being this close to another person.

All too soon, the pressure began to build as Blake learned how she liked to be touched. A little harder there, a bit softer that way.

She was groaning and barely able to focus on kissing him as the orgasm crashed over her, sending pleasure throughout her entire body.

And just as she hovered on the edge of so much pleasure it hurt, Blake stilled, and another wave crashed over her.

She did cry out then, but Blake kept his mouth on hers, caressing her all the while.

When she finally came down and slumped against the bed, boneless, he broke the kiss and murmured, "You're about to meet my dragon now."

In the next second, she was on her stomach, her hips raised, and a huskier version of Blake's voice said, "You're mine. All mine. And now I'm going to claim you."

DAMN, sex with Dawn was unlike anything Blake had ever experienced. And not just because she was interested in him for more than a chance at touching his dragon's lucky spot.

No, she tasted so bloody good, felt good, and made him want to do more than merely fuck her.

He wanted to taste her, cherish her, hold her close, and never let go.

However, as soon as he and Dawn finished their orgasms, his dragon roared, pushed to the front of his mind, and took control.

If it were normal circumstances, Blake could wrestle it back since mentally he was the slightly stronger of the two. However, his dragon was determined to claim Dawn and try to get her pregnant because she was their true mate. And if Blake tried to fight his beast to keep control over him, then the whole thing could backfire.

In other words, his dragon could keep Dawn all to himself for the entire frenzy. And there was no bloody way he was going to allow that to happen.

So he watched as his beast turned Dawn over, lifted her hips, and say, "You're mine. All mine. And now I'm going to claim you."

She arched her back, and both man and beast groaned. Their human wanted all of them and wasn't running for the hills.

His dragon entered her swiftly and pumped their hips, murmuring over and over again, "My female. Mine."

Given how his beast was usually more levelheaded, the instinctual mutterings were a bit of a surprise.

He said to his beast, *Remember, she's human. Don't break her.*

She can handle it. Look how she moves with me. She wants it.

Dawn moaned, and Blake wished he could hold her close and capture the sound with his mouth.

Still, it gave him the chance to watch her lovely arse as she moved, longing for the day he could hold her against him, feel that softness against his dick, and fall asleep.

It would be like heaven.

He mentally blinked. He'd turned into a bloody romantic. Who would've guessed that could ever happen?

His dragon roared and, with each thrust, said a word. "You. Are. Mine. Always."

Then his beast stilled as pleasured exploded throughout their body, his dick spending inside Dawn's core and sending her into her own orgasm.

When she'd wrung every last drop from their dick, Blake said to his beast, *My turn. She needs to rest a little.*

She can take more. She doesn't carry our baby yet. She must, then she'll carry our scent and keep the other males away.

Just a little rest. She needs it. Unless you want to scare her away?

His dragon finally grunted. *A short one. But then we claim her again.*

Deal.

His dragon receded to the back of his mind, and Blake took control again.

He leaned down to kiss Dawn's shoulder and said, "Are you okay?"

She glanced over her shoulder to meet his gaze.

"More than okay. And it's strange, but I can tell you and dragon apart fairly easily."

Wanting more than sex, he sat and turned her until Dawn sat in his lap, facing him. He traced her cheek, down her neck, and lightly played with her nipple. "He's usually a bit more normal sounding. But as the frenzy wears on, he'll get more and more frantic. I hope you're prepared."

She looped her arms around his neck, a wicked gleam in her eyes. "More than prepared—I'm looking forward to it."

He snorted. "So it just took good sex to win you over to the dragon-shifter side then?"

She grinned, the sight making his heart skip a beat. "It doesn't hurt."

She tilted her head, her hair brushing her shoulder. This time, he reached up to play with the blonde strands, loving how soft they were. "And humans say dragon-shifters are bad when it comes to sex."

She leaned over and whispered dramatically, "I think it's a distraction tactic, personally. To hide some secret sex dungeon in their shed or something."

He laughed, trying to imagine a human couple sneaking off to said shed. "No need for a shed. Once the frenzy has passed, I'd much rather go searching for a spot in the woods with you."

She traced his jaw. "You'll ruin your recluse reputation soon enough with me, won't you?"

He hugged her closer until her front pressed against his. "I'm more than willing to let it go for you."

As she searched his gaze, Blake felt the stirring of his

dragon waking up from a power nap. *Why are you talking? Breaks are for food, not chatting. Hurry up and ensure she still has energy. I want her again.*

Blake resisted a sigh and said to Dawn, "My dragon is even more eager than you to keep this frenzy going. So if you need food or anything important, now's the time to do it."

She wiggled in his lap, his cock already hardening again. "Right now, I just want more of you, Blake. So kiss me again."

And without another word, he crushed his lips to hers and focused on learning all the best ways to please his human. At least when he was in control. His dragon had his own brand of magic that seemed to make Dawn happy, too.

Chapter Ten

As Dawn blinked her eyes against the bright light, she tried to remember what day it was. Had another passed? She'd long ago lost count. Not because she didn't enjoy the frenzy, but each day made her wonder if the dragons had been wrong about her being able to conceive again.

Then a familiar warm hand caressed her cheek, and she turned over to meet Blake's gaze. His sleep-husky voice rolled over her. "Good morning, love."

Noting how his pupils weren't flashing, she wondered how long Blake would be in charge this time. However, first things first—she needed food if she was to keep up with her dragonman. "Ready for breakfast?"

She moved to get up, but Blake pulled her down and turned her so he could put her back against his front. As he kissed her neck, she asked, "Again?"

He held her a few beats before his hand moved to her lower abdomen. Her heart beat faster, wondering if it were true. He finally whispered, "Not until you're fully rested, Dawn. You have to protect our child and be strong for him or her."

For a second, she lay there stunned. She'd wanted to believe Bram and the others that miracles could happen between true mates, but Dawn had always had a small bit of doubt, too. More than one doctor had claimed to have a surefire way to give her a child in the long road to having Daisy, and she'd learned to be a bit skeptical.

But Blake's hand was warm against her belly, and she tentatively placed her own over his. "Is it really true?"

Her voice cracked at the end, and Blake's concerned voice filled her ear. "Are you okay, Dawn? Should I fetch the doctor?"

Even though tears trailed down her cheeks, she shook her head. "No, no, I'm good. More than good, actually."

She turned until she could face him. Blake instantly frowned, and his gaze turned concerned. "You're crying, love. Why?"

She wiped a hand across her eyes before answering. "They're happy tears, I assure you. I just didn't know if it could happen. I know everyone said it can with true mates, but I guess I still doubted it."

He kissed her gently on the lips and then said, "If you need to hear it from Dr. Sid, I can take you to the surgery straightaway."

She kissed him a few beats before laying her forehead against his. "No, if your dragon says it's true, then I believe him."

He rolled onto his back and brought her against his chest. He stroked her back as he murmured against her hair, "It's true, Dawn. My scent is mixed with yours, which means you carry my babe. Of course, with my necessary part finished now, I'm going to need your help because I don't know the first thing about taking care of a baby."

She smiled and snuggled against his hard, warm chest, loving how his scent had already become familiar to her. "I'll show you the ropes. And I imagine Daisy will want to help, too."

At the mention of her daughter, a longing crashed over her. She missed Daisy, more than she'd realized.

As if reading her thoughts, Blake said, "Once we eat and shower, we'll go see Bram. That way he can get everything in motion to bring Daisy here as soon as possible."

Leaning back, she met his gaze again. "I'm happy right now, I truly am. So please don't take this the wrong way, but can I call Daisy soon, too? I need to hear her voice."

He stroked her cheek. "Of course you do. The frenzy took fifteen days, and I don't think you've ever been out of contact with her that long, have you?"

She shook her head. "No, never."

"Well, then let's get up and put things in motion so you can speak with her."

As Dawn stared into Blake's eyes, she didn't detect any hint of resentment. The problem was she didn't know if it was because he was good at hiding it or because he truly understood how much Dawn loved her daughter.

The frenzy had been a sort of bubble, one where it'd

been just her and Blake. She only hoped that it wouldn't burst completely when Daisy entered because it would break her heart to have her daughter and the father of her second child at odds with one another.

No, Dawn. Stop it. She was so used to things going wrong with men that she was poisoning her own mind. Blake would have his chance, and she'd see for herself how it went.

Although was it too much to ask for a man she could probably fall in love with as well as a happy, blended family?

Kissing Blake one last time, she got out of bed and went about getting ready. Dawn wasn't a coward, so the only thing to do was put everything in motion so she could find out what her future held next.

Chapter Eleven

B lake did his best to hide how nervous he was, which meant keeping his expression sort of friendly and not tapping his hand against his thigh.

He wasn't anxious because he would soon be moving in with an eleven-year-old girl who would be his stepdaughter, though. He knew that would be a challenge, and he accepted it in order for a chance with Dawn.

No, he was nervous because he was about to show Dawn his dragon form for the first time.

He could already see a few people at the edges of the lesser-used landing area situated toward the rear of Stonefire's land. Somehow word had already traveled about him wanting to shift, and spectators had flocked to the area.

His dragon grunted. *It doesn't matter. This is for Dawn and only Dawn. Besides, this is our last chance to show her our dragon form before Daisy arrives tomorrow morning.*

I know, but if someone rushes out to touch our black spot and starts to make a dramatic wish, I'm not sure I want to stay in our dragon form and let Dawn see the embarrassment.

Before his beast could argue further, Dawn walked into the landing area with Sasha at her side, and he forgot about everything but his soon-to-be mate.

Ever since he'd woken up and known she carried his child, she'd glowed. While he hoped it was partially because of him, he knew it was probably because she was so happy to have another child.

His beast sighed. *Stop with the doubting. She went through the frenzy, embraced both of us, and has been nothing but open and teasing since.*

It was true—the last day, ever since they'd finally emerged from their cottage, had been full of congratulations and stolen glances at one another.

He finally replied, *I know. It's just shifting in public always shakes me up a bit. I don't think I'll ever get used to spectators.*

Then Dawn walked up to him, touched his cheek, his nervousness faded significantly. She said, "You should've waited for me and then we could've walked here together."

He kept his voice low so that only Dawn could hear it. "I needed a little time to prepare. And I knew you were with Sasha anyway."

She searched his gaze and finally leaned over and kissed him gently. "Still, next time, talk to me about it, okay? If we're to make a family, we need to be open about everything."

Tracing her jaw, he nodded. "I'll try, I promise. Just remember I've been a bachelor for nearly forty years so it's going to take a little time to adjust."

The corner of her mouth ticked up. "Oh, just wait until Daisy gets here. Then you won't have a spare moment to worry about it."

The comment would've concerned him even three weeks ago. But now? It just reminded him that he no longer had to live alone and isolate himself any longer. After the mating ceremony the next day, he'd have a mate and a new daughter.

Two people who would get to know the real him and not merely the fact he was a unicorn dragon.

Blake kissed Dawn's cheek and motioned toward where Sasha stood, at the edge of the landing area, near the six-foot-high rock walls filled with cubbies for clothing and items. "Speaking of which, I want to make sure you can see and touch my dragon before we're dragged into more paperwork and planning for tomorrow. Between Daisy's arrival and the mating ceremony, we won't have a spare moment after this for a while. So you should go stand by Sasha so I can shift."

She touched his cheek one last time—he would never tire of her soft, warm touch—and then went to stand by her friend.

Once Dawn was in place, Blake focused solely on his female. None of the other dragon-shifters lingering about mattered.

His dragon grunted. *Good. Then let's get started.*

Blake quickly shed his clothes and tossed them to the side—he'd opted to not stand naked waiting for Dawn since the human was adjusting to the idea of casual nudity—and closed his eyes to concentrate.

He imagined wings sprouting from his back, his nose

elongating into a snout, and his form growing and stretching until he finally stood in his large dragon form.

With a deep inhalation, he opened his eyes and found Dawn's gaze.

She stood in awe, and it took an elbow jab from Sasha to break the spell.

As she walked slowly toward him, Blake noticed from the corner of his eyes that a few people moved closer toward him.

His dragon spoke up. *Ignore them. Dawn is all that matters.*

And he did exactly that, watching the play of emotions over her face as she drew closer. The awe was soon replaced with wonder and then curiosity.

Since he couldn't talk in his dragon form, Blake lowered his head so that when Dawn was near enough, he could gently bump her shoulder.

She laughed at the contact and then raised a hand to touch his snout. Her voice chased away his annoyance at a few teenagers edging ever closer to his tail. She said, "I'm not sure how else to say it, but you're beautiful, Blake."

As she stroked his snout, his dragon hummed. The sound made Dawn smile even wider.

His beast said, *See? Only Dawn matters. And she thinks I'm beautiful.*

I know, and you're never going to forget to remind me of that, are you?

Of course not.

As his human stroked upward, toward his ear, Blake lowered his head more. Then she found the patch of skin without scales behind his ear and focused her attention there. As he leaned into her caress, he knew she must've received some hints from Sasha about what to do.

Then he felt someone touching his tail, where his spot was, and he froze.

Dawn must've noticed the tensing of his muscles because she leaned to the side and frowned. She shouted, "It's not polite to touch someone without permission. Would you want someone grabbing your tail in front of your friends or mate?"

The touch vanished, and a surly teenage voice filled his ears. "No."

"Right, then be off and leave him alone."

He glanced over his shoulder, and to Blake's surprise, the teenagers were grumbling but walking away.

Dawn patted his side. "I will never have your strength, speed, or super senses, but I can certainly try to get the children to leave you alone. It may not always work, but there's almost a 'mother tone' that seems to work on a lot of kids. So I'll try my best, and I'm sure Daisy will help me chase off the unwanted attention, too. She'll take the responsibility very seriously, I think."

If he could've smiled in his dragon form, he would have. The thought of Dawn and Daisy shooing away unwanted spectators was too amusing.

His dragon spoke up. *See? She is perfect for us in so many ways, much more than the fact she's so open in bed and can even make you laugh when no one else can.*

Sasha's voice broke through his conversation. "Dawn, I hate to break this up, but we have that meeting at the school soon. I'll give you and Blake a few minutes alone and wait just outside the wall here." The dark-haired dragonwoman shot a few glances at the lingering dragon-shifters. "We will *all* give them some privacy, won't we?"

With a few grumbles, the others left. Sasha winked and also disappeared beyond the wall surrounding the landing area.

His beast huffed. *Why do we have to change back so soon? I want more ear scratches.*

There's a lot to do before Daisy gets here tomorrow. Besides, wouldn't you like to have both Dawn and Daisy scratching behind your ears?

Maybe. His beast paused before adding, *Fine, shift back. But don't make excuses when I want to shift again in front of Dawn. I want more time with her.*

He gently bumped Dawn's shoulder and motioned with his head for her to move back. With one last pat to his snout, she moved to a safe enough distance away.

Blake imagined his limbs shrinking, his wings melding into his back, and his face returning to normal. As soon as he was once again in his human form, he strode right up to Dawn. Not caring who saw, he hauled her against his body and kissed her.

Her noise of surprise quickly morphed into the soft sounds she made as she kissed him back. He licked and devoured her mouth, tangling his tongue with hers when he could. He finally let her up for air and cupped her cheek. He murmured, "Thank you."

She tilted her head. "It's nothing, really. I remember when I was pregnant and everyone would just touch my belly without asking. It gets irritating rather quickly. I figured it's the same for your spot, right? You just need a little Dawn and Daisy to remind people it's not okay to break personal boundaries simply because someone believes a story."

He chuckled. "The Dawn and Daisy squad, huh? I don't think anyone will stand a chance."

She grinned. "Not if Daisy is involved. I'm sure she'll want T-shirts and will make posters or something, to post all around the landing areas with various kinds of warnings."

As he stared into Dawn's eyes, matching her smile, something shifted inside him.

His human had come to mean so much to him so quickly. He was more than halfway in love with her.

His dragon growled. *She is ours. I hope you treasure her as she deserves.*

Blake would always try. But first things first, he needed to ensure everything was ready for Daisy's arrival the next day.

So he kissed his beautiful mate quickly, dressed, and took her hand as he led her toward the school. Much like she'd had his back at the landing area, he'd have hers for all aspects of clan life that were new to her.

Maybe with his actions, he could prove how much he wanted her.

And so Blake helped in every way he could for the remainder of the day, not even disappointed when Dawn was so exhausted she merely fell asleep in his arms later that night. Simply holding his true mate was enough.

Chapter Twelve

Just before noon the next day, Dawn walked out of Bram's cottage with Blake at her side and was instantly accosted in a hug by her daughter.

After a second of confusion since she'd thought Daisy would wait for them inside the main Protector's building, she held Daisy tightly against her. "Daisy, you're here. I've missed you."

Daisy looked up at her and bobbed her head. "Yes, they said I had to wait outside until you were done. Something about you doing something important."

She brushed some of Daisy's wild hair from her face. "I had to sign some things to make sure we can live on Stonefire."

"So, it's all done? It should be moving day soon, right? Mrs. Barlow only let me pack one suitcase, but that's not all my stuff. And I couldn't bring all my stories and books about dragons with me, either. Which I need since I think they're going to be really important."

She laughed. "We'll be moving for good in the next few days. You'll survive without the rest of your stuff until then." She looked up and smiled at Mariana and Freddie. "Thanks for looking after her, Mari."

Mariana's English was teased with her Portuguese roots. "No problem. My Emily loved having a friend around. Although I think my son is happy she's gone."

Daisy's voice prevented Dawn from replying. "It was fun, Mum. But you had fun, too, right? And now I'll have a little brother and sister? And Mr. Whitby will live with us, too?"

Right, Blake. The man was a little nervous about first living with Daisy, and here Dawn had forgotten to include him.

She really needed to remember it wasn't just her and Daisy anymore.

However, Blake spoke before Dawn could say a word. "Call me Blake, Daisy. And yes to both questions—we'll all be living together from now on, and in about nine months, you'll have a sibling."

Dawn bit back a smile at how formal Blake sounded. He may like to help out at the school, but he clearly wasn't used to talking with kids on a regular basis. Dawn jumped in. "How about we all go visit our new home together? I heard that Freddie's mum should be there with some biscuits and cake."

Her daughter jumped back and clapped her hands. "Biscuits and cake? Are they a special dragon-shifter recipe? I had some last time I was here, but I can't remember the name. Do you remember, Freddie?"

The little boy grunted. "Ginger dragon biscuits."

"Right, ginger dragon biscuits. Did she make them this time, too, Freddie? Or maybe a special type of dragon cake instead? There might even be a yummy drink I've never tried before. There are so many possibilities now that I live with a dragon clan!"

Dawn laughed and decided that if she didn't start steering them all in the right direction, Daisy could go on about treat possibilities for a good half hour. "How about we go and find out? That's much faster than if you keep guessing."

Freddie looked at Dawn. "Can I take her ahead? I promise we won't wander off."

She eyed the young dragon-shifter a second before nodding. "No wandering. Or else I hear your uncle will pay a visit to remind you of the clan rules."

Freddie sighed. "I don't want another lecture from Uncle Zain." He took Daisy's hand. "Come on, Daisy. We can pick out the best pieces for ourselves if we get there first."

Before she could say they needed to wait until everyone arrived before eating anything, Freddie and Daisy were already running down the footpath.

Blake spoke up. "Don't worry, Dawn. If there are treats involved, children usually follow the rules. Or, so it's been that way at the school events."

She smiled at Blake and desperately wanted to ask him if he was doing okay so far. However, she couldn't just let Mariana stand there by herself. So Dawn looked at the woman and said, "You're welcome to stay for tea and cake, Mari, if you like."

Mariana shook her head, her dark hair swinging

about her shoulders. "No, I need to drive back to Manchester before my children get off school."

Dawn walked up to Mariana and took one of her hands. "Thank you so much, Mari. And as soon as we're all set up here, you have to come visit."

Mariana gave a small smile. Dawn couldn't recall ever seeing her fully grin. All thanks to her ex-husband and his abuse, no doubt. The lingering effects had made the woman cautious, to the point Mariana had never allowed them to be closer than parents of two children who were friends.

Maybe she could find someone for Mariana on Stonefire. Not for purely selfish reasons, either, although Dawn would love to have someone from her old life around. Not to mention Emily was friends with Freddie and Daisy, too.

Mariana replied, "Emily would love that. I'm sure they'll want to set it up soon. Call me when everything has settled down."

She nodded and wished she could hug the woman. However, Mariana was careful never to touch anyone but her children. So Dawn merely replied, "Of course."

After a few more details were sorted and Mariana was escorted away toward her car, Dawn looked up at Blake as she took his hand. "Ready to start our new life?"

"Mostly. But for you, I'd do anything."

His words rang with truth, and it made her heart squeeze a little. She really hoped he could handle Daisy because it was becoming harder to imagine spending her life with any other man. "Well, then let's go. Otherwise,

I'm afraid Daisy will sweet talk Sasha and eat four pieces of cake before we get there."

He chuckled and tugged her along the path. "Then let's hurry. I know what sugar does to children, and I'd rather not have my first night as a stepfather be dealing with a sugar rush and the ensuing crash."

"It'd be a good introduction, for sure." He raised his eyebrows, and she laughed. "Okay, not even I want to deal with it." She released his hand. "So I'll race you there."

She took off down the pathway, trying to run despite the fact she was most assuredly not a runner, and loved how, when Blake caught up with her, he snatched her from behind and twirled her a second before putting her down.

As they walked quickly together hand in hand, for once, Dawn merely focused on being happy and pushing her worries aside.

BLAKE LOVED CATCHING Dawn and being playful with her. It was something he never would've thought of doing before a human female had shown him how little, pointless games or actions could be so much fun.

Now the question was whether he could do that with Daisy, too, and not have it be weird.

His dragon spoke up. *Stop worrying so much. You've seen how parents act with their kids at the various school events you've helped with over the years. Try being less formal, for a start. I don't think Daisy is the type of child to respond well to that.*

As if it were as easy as watching kids at a school event. *Except this isn't a child we'll see one night and then go home. If she doesn't like us from the beginning, it'll break Dawn's heart.*

Then loosen up and win Daisy over.

His dragon had always been the more laidback out of the two of them. No doubt he reveled in the fact he could teach Blake something. *You're loving this, aren't you?*

His beast snorted. *Of course I am. And not just because we have a female of our own now, either. But you might actually have to take advice from me on how to handle Daisy.*

He muttered a few words inside his head but didn't get to do more than that because their new home came into view.

It was a two-story cottage with a small garden in the back. While not as isolated as his previous home, it was toward the edge of the main living area. They'd had two choices of houses, but this one was closer to the Atherton place, and he and Dawn had agreed it would be best for Daisy and Freddie.

Dawn squeezed his hand, garnering his attention. "And so our new life begins. Ready for the adventure?"

"More than anything."

Her cheeks flushed, and it made both man and beast happy.

She lightly swatted his side. "Stop with the hyperbole, Blake. Or better yet, save it for your conversations with Daisy. She loves them, and the more over the top, the better. I'm sure before long it'll turn into a contest of sorts between you two."

He wanted to say it wasn't hyperbole but decided to

merely nod. After all, he didn't know if Dawn already felt as connected to him as he was to her. "I'm used to giving the facts, but I'll try my best."

She kissed his cheek. "Right, then let's see if Daisy has managed to sweet talk herself into extra cake or if Sasha was able to resist her."

They approached the door, and he noticed the little metal plaque that said, "The Chadwick-Whitbys." Dawn had wanted to keep both names because of her daughter, and he'd hadn't minded.

However, seeing the plaque really made everything real. His new path would start as soon as he stepped inside their home. "Sasha must've brought that," he stated.

Dawn bobbed her head. "She did say she had a few surprises for us. It's lovely, isn't it? Now, let's see what else she put together."

They entered the cottage and were instantly greeted with laughter and chatter from the kitchen. Like most homes on Stonefire, they had some soundproofing to keep neighbors and passersby from hearing everything that went on since dragon-shifters had supersensitive hearing.

As soon as they entered the kitchen, Blake smiled at Daisy dancing around the room, performing one of the routines she'd done in the play. When she noticed them, she stopped and grinned. "Mum, there's so much more room here. I can even dance in the kitchen, unlike our place back in Manchester."

He shot Dawn a questioning look, and she shrugged

one shoulder. "We've always rented a flat. You'll see when we move everything in a few days."

He'd agreed to visit a city for the very first time to help his new mate and daughter pack and move.

Before meeting Dawn, he would've cringed at the idea. But his mate was human, and his offspring would be half-human, and so he needed to learn more about her world no matter how loud or smelly a big place like Manchester might be for a dragon-shifter.

Daisy jumped in again. "Hey, Mum, can we go see my room now? Mrs. Atherton said we had to wait for you to get here before I could go upstairs. She even hinted that she left a surprise or two inside my room. So can we go now, Mum? Please?"

Dawn smiled. "The three of us will go check it out. If that's okay, Sasha?"

Sasha bobbed her head. "I need Freddie to help me with the sandwiches anyway." She winked. "I'll listen for the squeals."

His dragon spoke up. *Okay, now I'm curious, too. Let's hurry. I hope Sasha didn't outdo the gifts we bought for Daisy.*

To say an inner dragon was competitive was an understatement. *I don't think she'd do that. Regardless, she only bought things out of love for Daisy. And she needs all the allies on Stonefire she can muster.*

His dragon harrumphed. *But she's not going to be Daisy's parent from now on. We should get the extra points for it.*

Blake did his best not to laugh at his beast's surly tone.

Thankfully Dawn motioned for them to head upstairs. She took the lead with Daisy right behind her, and Blake brought up the rear. They soon stopped in front of the bedroom door the farthest away from his and Dawn's, which was Daisy's room.

His female put her hand on the doorknob but didn't turn it. "Hey, how about a game, Daisy? You can try to guess what's inside. If, after ten guesses, you still don't figure it out, we'll go in."

Daisy sighed. "Mum, don't make me wait. That could take ages. And I've been waiting forever to come back here. You've already seen it, so it's only fair I can see my new room, too."

Dawn smiled. "But I thought you liked games? You always go on about wanting to play more of them."

"But not right now. Freddie hinted at some surprises days and days ago. I've been so patient, but I'm about to burst if I don't find out what's in there, Mum."

As Daisy slumped forward, Dawn laughed, and even Blake smiled. Daisy did indeed have a flair for the dramatic.

His female turned the knob. "We can't have that happen, now, can we? Let's see what's in here…"

As soon as Dawn cleared the door, Daisy ran inside and screamed. "Look! There are dragons painted on the walls." Blake was glad she liked the mural a colleague of his had painted and watched as Daisy raced to the small bookshelf next to the desk they'd picked for her. "And there are loads of stories with dragon in the title. Some I haven't read yet." Then she went to the bed, and Blake finally noticed what Sasha had brought.

Daisy lifted one and then another stuffed dragon. The larger one was white with a black spot, and the smaller stuffed dragon was blue. She held up the white one. "This is you, right, Blake? I know I haven't seen your dragon, but I've heard about him. And now you'll help guard my room, right?" She hugged both of them to her chest. "And the other must be Freddie. They're perfect."

He spoke to his beast. *See? She likes them a lot. You can't be mad about Sasha's surprise.*

Maybe.

Daisy then raced up to him and Dawn. "I love my room! Did you decorate it together? Can we have dragons painted on the walls downstairs, too? And are there more books to get? There's so much to learn to catch up to everyone else."

Blake smiled. "I'm sure you'll catch up. Although I can always help tutor, if you like."

She beamed up at him. "Oh, I'll need your help, for sure. Maybe not today because there's more to see and there's a big party tonight, right? So you guys can get married. No, I mean mated. That's right. I need to use the right words."

Dawn brushed back some hair from her daughter's face. "Since we don't have a lot of time before Blake and I have to get ready, let's head downstairs and spend some time with Sasha and Freddie, okay? And make sure to thank her for your dragons."

"Oh, I will! My new dragons should come eat with us."

Dawn shook her head. "No, they stay up here. Otherwise, they'll be covered in icing within thirty seconds."

"I'm not that messy, Mum." Dawn raised her brows,

and Daisy sighed as she trudged back to her bed. "Fine, I'll leave them up here."

Blake hesitated a second, afraid he might be bumping in, but decided to speak up. "I have something more interesting for you downstairs, anyway, Daisy. It's a special dragon-shifter drink that also has some interesting science behind it."

A lot of kids would groan or paste fake smiles, but Daisy stood tall again, curiosity in her gaze.

Yes, this young human female would be trouble when she got older, if they weren't careful.

Daisy raced up to him and took his hand. "Then let's go, Blake. I need to know everything I can about dragon-shifters. So start teaching me."

Dawn chuckled, and he shared an amused glance with his female.

And as Daisy led him down the stairs, he thought that maybe things would be okay in the end.

His dragon snorted. *Until you run out of interesting dragon facts for her.*

Shut it, dragon. I'll never run out of things to teach her.

If you say so.

Ignoring his dragon, Blake merely enjoyed teaching Freddie and Daisy the special drink that doubled in size when adding the right ingredients.

While usually he was a long-term planner—his research required that type of mindset—Blake was going to just enjoy the moment and try his hardest to make more of them until it seemed natural that they were a family.

Chapter Thirteen

A couple of hours later, as the front door clicked closed behind Dawn, Blake took a deep breath and headed back toward the kitchen. Daisy was singing some song he didn't know and thumbing through one of her new books.

He stopped in the doorway and tried not to breathe too hard lest he disturb her.

His dragon sighed. *We only have to watch her for an hour or so. It's not the end of the world.*

While Blake knew that, this would be the first time he was alone with Daisy and entirely responsible for her care. Still, Dawn wanted Sasha to help her get ready for the mating ceremony, and this was his first duty to prove how much he wanted Dawn—and Daisy—in his life.

Taking a deep breath, he walked up to Daisy, and she glanced up. "Is this book true? Did dragon-shifters used to fight humans a long time ago, back when they used horses and swords and stuff?"

Blake nodded and sat across from her at the table. "You've learned a little about wars in school, right?"

She scrunched up her nose in thought. "A little. Some lasted a really long time, I think."

"Well, it's the same for dragon-shifters—we've been in wars, too. Sometimes with other dragons, sometimes with humans, and sometimes with both humans and dragons who teamed up together."

Daisy tilted her head. "But not now, right? I mean, I see dragon-shifters on TV sometimes being interviewed by human reporters. And you wouldn't be mating my mum, either, if we were at war."

He debated on how honest he should be but decided Daisy was old enough to learn a little. "Well, there's not a full-scale war, no. But dragon hunters want to kill us and drain us of our blood. So it's like a small war, I suppose."

"Why don't you just share your blood for free with people who need it? Then maybe they wouldn't try to hunt dragons for it."

While simple on the surface, Blake took a second to think about how to explain that dragon-shifters needed some advantages to avoid becoming permanent second-class citizens to humans.

He finally settled on saying, "Well, people might then get greedy. And then dragons could end up being weak all the time from giving so much blood. And if we didn't have enough? People would get mad at us anyway."

"Well, maybe there's a way to use science to help everyone. You always say it can do a lot of good things. Many times it almost seems like magic, but there's really some special recipe involved, right?"

He smiled. "So you were paying attention during the special dragon camp sessions then."

She sat up tall and bobbed her head. "Of course. I try to listen to everything the dragons say. I'm not sure what I want to do when I grow up yet, but it'll probably be something related to dragon-shifters. And so I need to learn it all."

He chuckled. "We can never learn everything."

"Well, I'm going to try."

As they smiled at one another, Blake's nervousness faded away. If nothing else, he could always use learning as a way to bond with his soon-to-be-stepdaughter.

Then Daisy frowned and blurted, "Are you going to leave like my dad did?"

He blinked at the sudden change of subject. He hadn't expected that question, or at least this soon.

She continued before he could say anything. "It's just that I like you, and my mum really likes you, and I don't want her to be sad anymore. And somehow I think she'll be sad if you leave. She's such a great mum and should be happy instead."

His dragon said softly, *We won't leave. Make sure she knows that.*

Daisy spoke again. "So your dragon just talked, right, since your eyes flashed? What did he say?"

Blake wanted to lay his hand on Daisy's to maybe keep her from talking but didn't know if she would be comfortable with that yet. So instead, he merely said, "Yes, my dragon talks a lot. So asking all the time might be a little time-consuming." She opened her mouth, but he didn't let her get a word in. "As for leaving—you, your mum, and any other children she has will always be a part of my life. Stonefire is my home and I won't leave it."

Not exactly a declaration of staying together forever, but Blake and Dawn hadn't even said they loved each other yet. Blake loved his human, but he wouldn't assume anything about her feelings.

But he would always be in their lives, even if it were solely for the sake of their child. That was the truth.

Daisy stared a second before nodding. "I believe you. Which is good because if you leave, then I'll also be stuck with all the babysitting."

He chuckled. "There are plenty of people here to help your mother any way she needs it. I know it's been just you and her for a long time, but it doesn't have to be that way anymore."

Unusual for her, Daisy remained quiet a few beats, merely staring at him. She finally nodded. "I believe you, Blake."

His dragon spoke up. *She will be a good older sister to our child. Everyone dismisses her as flighty and hyperactive, but she can be serious and pensive at times, too.*

I agree. I think even I misjudged her a little.

Daisy stared at him as she wiggled in her seat, no doubt itching to ask him about his dragon. She really did want to know everything.

Then Blake noticed the time and decided their serious conversation would need to be put on hold. He stood. "We'll have to talk some more later. Right now, we both need to change clothes and head toward the great hall."

He half expected Daisy to resist, but she was out of her chair and running up the stairs in the blink of an eye. "Hurry, Blake! I want to see everyone dressed up. Because of the outfits, I can stare—er, look at—all the tattoos!"

Shaking his head, he smiled as Daisy's bedroom door slammed shut.

He hurried up the stairs to his room, wanting to ensure he was ready before Daisy.

And as he changed clothes for his mating ceremony, he thought maybe, just maybe, he would get the hang of being a father to an older child. While there was a lot of ground to still cover, he'd survived his first test.

But within minutes, Daisy banged on the door, asking for him to hurry up, and he pushed aside all the serious thoughts to finish getting ready for his own mating ceremony.

Which was something he never thought he'd have, and he'd never take for granted.

Dawn stood in a room off the main floor of the great hall, Sasha plucking at a few bits of Dawn's hair. Her friend finally stepped back and nodded. "There you go. Now Blake will want to do the frenzy all over again."

Damn her cheeks, they heated. "Since Daisy is staying with us now, we can't be that, er, loud."

Sasha laughed. "Oh, I'm sure you'll get creative. Just because I had kids didn't mean I gave up my kinky bed play."

As her friend winked, Dawn lightly hit her arm. "Stop it, Sasha. What if Daisy walked in right now?"

She motioned toward the door with her head. "She's out in the hall with Freddie, Alfie, and Evie. If anyone can distract Daisy and keep her in the great hall, Evie can."

Dawn raised her brows. "Just because she's the clan leader's mate doesn't guarantee that."

"All she has to do is promise a tour of the Protector's building, and I'm sure Daisy will do anything."

She sighed. "Everyone making deals is going to backfire on me someday, I'm sure of it."

"It won't last forever. For now, it's just a way to try and help Daisy feel welcome. And besides, she arrived dressed and ready, which means Blake passed the first parent test. I wonder if he made a deal, too, or tried something else?"

Since Dawn could barely contain Daisy's wild, curly hair, she hadn't frowned at the slightly wilder look Daisy had arrived with. "Yes, he got her here on time and ready. Although I hate to think of it as a series of tests. Because that makes it seem as if Daisy isn't so much a person as an obstacle. And that isn't the way to start a family."

Sasha took a step closer. "Don't worry, Dawn. It's clear Blake adores you. He won't give up on Daisy. He's far more honorable than your ex."

She searched her friend's gaze. "I know that, but it's still hard for me to believe sometimes. I hope this uncertain feeling wears off eventually."

Sasha patted her arm. "It will, I just know it. You

deserve some happiness, Dawn. Stop trying to find excuses as to why you don't."

As she stared in the brown eyes of her friend—her best friend, really—she didn't hold back. "I know. Although once her paternal aunt finds out about what's happened, my happy ending may be not quite perfect. I'm almost positive she'll voice her distrust of dragons much louder than normal, maybe even to Daisy herself. However, since she's the only family Daisy knows on her father's side, I don't want to just cut her out of Daisy's life. I'm not sure what to do."

Sasha waved a hand in dismissal. "If she's afraid of dragon-shifters, that's her problem. Besides, if Daisy can't convince her aunt to change her mind, no one could. It'll be the aunt's loss, not Daisy's." She motioned toward the door. "But enough about a distant relative in a city some- where. I hear Bram telling everyone to get into place, which is our cue. Are you ready to go?"

With a deep breath, she nodded, and they walked out of the room toward the side entrance of the great hall. It was time to make her second chance at a family official.

BLAKE STOOD inside the doorway off the left side of the dais in the great hall, waiting for his signal to go on stage.

His gaze kept checking to make sure Daisy was still in the room, but she hadn't left Freddie's side since they'd arrived.

His dragon spoke up. *She wouldn't miss this. It's her first dragon mating ceremony.*

I want to believe that, but she has a reputation for sneaking out when no one is watching.

Well, she now has us and Dawn—not to mention most of the clan—watching her. Before she was merely a visitor, but no longer. Stonefire won't let anything happen to her.

He was about to say that might not be enough when Dawn emerged from the opposite side of the dais, and any thoughts unrelated to his human fled his mind.

She wore the dark red color of Stonefire, her dress fastened over one shoulder and flowing down her body. Even though it wasn't form-fitting, both man and beast mentally growled at how revealing it could be, showing off the curves of her body.

Then Dawn caught his gaze, smiled, and his feet moved of their own accord toward her. They met in the middle of the dais, right in front of a tall table with a box holding their mating bands, and he took her hand. He murmured, "You look beautiful."

While not as deep a blush as she'd had many times during the frenzy, they tinged pink. "You aren't too bad yourself."

He resisted adjusting the sash across his bare chest. His dragon whispered, *Remember, humans don't walk around mostly bare-chested that often this far north.*

Ignoring his dragon, he kissed the back of Dawn's hand right before Bram's voice boomed inside the large hall. Everyone quieted down as he said, "Today is truly a special event. After all, it's been such a long time since Stonefire welcomed a mother and daughter pair to the clan. I hope that everyone will help Dawn and Daisy adjust and remember that from today, they will be part of our clan, too."

There were a few claps and a whistle from somewhere. Regardless, Blake never looked away from Dawn's eyes.

Usually, mating ceremonies were only done between two people, but everyone had thought it a good idea to have Bram help in this case. That way, the clan would understand that Daisy may be a human child, but she was now part of Stonefire, with the complete backing of the clan leader.

Bram gestured toward Blake and Dawn. "And now we'll have our ceremony. Given how many we've had in recent years, I hope you can enjoy yet another one without getting too bored."

There were a few chuckles from the crowd because it was true. Blake had lost count of how many mating ceremonies he'd been forced to attend in the last two or three years.

His dragon huffed. *That doesn't matter right now. Start the ceremony. I want Dawn as our mate. Now.*

Since Blake was just as eager, he waited for Bram to descend the steps before he spoke up first. "Dawn Chadwick, our beginning was accidental and a surprise. However, you agreeing to be my mate is the best thing to ever happen to me. I always thought isolating myself would make me happy. Little did I know it only took the right female to make me realize I'd been hiding away from everything. But no longer. With you at my side, I can face anything. And whilst being a parent will be all new to me, I hope I can help with Daisy, too, and tell her all she wants to know about dragon-shifters. I love you, Dawn. Will you accept my mate claim?"

Blake had gone back and forth about saying I love you, but he meant it and didn't want to leave it out of such an important occasion.

Dawn replied, "I do."

He nearly exhaled in relief at her answer. Picking up the silver arm cuff engraved with his name in the old language, he slid it around her upper bicep.

She smiled at him and said, "Blake Whitby, you're right—our beginning was a little bit of a surprise. However, I'm glad it happened. You're smart, kind, and a very loving man. While I know our future is just starting, I truly believe it will be a good one. I care so much for you already and can't wait to write the rest of our story in the coming years. Will you accept my mate claim?"

He hid his disappointment at her lack of a love declaration, yet he respected her for being true to herself. It only made him more determined to win her heart completely.

"I do," he stated and offered the bicep without his dragon-shifter tattoo. As she slid the cool metal around his arm, he couldn't tear his gaze away from Dawn's. Once the band was in place, he pulled her close, cupped her cheek, and whispered for her ears only, "You're mine now, human," and kissed her.

He barely heard the cheers as he explored Dawn's mouth and reveled in the feel of her body against his.

She finally pulled back and murmured, "I'm sure Daisy will have some questions about that now."

He grinned. "Good."

And as he led his mate down the stairs toward the floor, where clan members were already lining up to congratulate them, he didn't think twice about the crowd of people. With his mate at his side and his new daughter racing toward them, Blake felt as if he could take on anything.

Funny how finding his true mate had changed his world so completely.

Chapter Fourteen

Two days later, Blake stared out the car window as Dawn turned off the motorway into a section of Manchester.

Ever since they'd left Stonefire, he'd watched as villages, towns, and cities grew larger the closer they got to the big metropolitan area.

But as his mate easily drove down the street through an area crowded cheek and jowl with buildings, he wondered how people could live this way.

His dragon spoke up. *Humans don't need areas to shift or fly. They can pack a lot of people in here. Besides, it's better than what it once was.*

Blake was no history teacher, but even he knew that the industrial revolution had dramatically transformed Manchester and the surrounding areas with factories and all sorts of new buildings. Not to mention the living conditions of the poor back then had been beyond his comprehension, and bad wasn't a strong enough word to describe the squalor. *Well, I'm just glad I don't have to live here. I can already hear a half-dozen conversations through the car window. Not to mention smells I don't even want to think about.*

His dragon snorted. *I'm sure once the tens of thousands of university students go home in the summer, it'll smell a lot better.*

Before he could debate that point, Daisy must've woken up from her nap because she shouted, "Look! There's my old school! We're nearly at our old flat, Blake."

The school building wasn't anything special, although truth be told, Blake didn't really pay attention to things such as architecture. He was more interested in the materials used to construct it.

Dawn soon parked on the street in front of a two-story house just as Daisy shouted, "We're here!"

It looked like a house, not a flat. "It's bigger than I thought it would be."

Dawn smiled and explained, "It's divided into four flats. Thankfully I was able to get a ground floor one so Daisy didn't have to worry about walking softly."

Humans really did like to live in close quarters. Putting four dragon-shifters, let alone families, in such close quarters would soon drive everyone mad.

His beast said, *Remember, humans don't hear or smell as well as we do. So it wouldn't bother them.*

I suppose. I guess I'm just used to more space since dragon clans are all designed that way.

Not to mention Blake had lived apart from even most of his own clan for years.

Dawn's voice halted his conversation with his dragon. "It looks like Jane and Rafe made it, too, with the van."

The human sibling pair had volunteered to help with the move. After all, having humans go into the city was a lot less paperwork.

Daisy asked, "Can I get out now, Mum? I want to show Blake our old place and tell him all the really good stories."

Dawn smiled at him. "It's up to Blake."

"Oh, Blake, can we go in now? Please?"

He turned halfway in his seat and smiled. One day soon, he'd need to learn to say no to Daisy, but today wasn't that day. He was still trying to get on her good side. "All right, but no running or shouting, okay?"

"Okay. Let's go!"

She exited the car and opened his door before he could blink. Dawn quickly handed him a set of keys, kissed his cheek, and murmured, "Have fun."

Daisy took his hand. "Come on, Blake. Hurry up. I want to show you everything before it all gets packed up."

Not wanting to draw attention from the neighbors, even if it was in the middle of the day during the week, Blake undid his seat belt and followed Daisy to the door. Her voice was almost at a normal level as she explained, "There are two doors. The front one and the inside one. I can do it for you, Blake. Give me the keys."

He did and watched as she quickly opened the door. The inside smelled of dust and humans.

But Daisy quickly went to a door on the right side and opened it with another key. She waved for him to follow. "In here, Blake. Come on."

The floor above him creaked, meaning someone was home. Not wanting to find out if they tolerated dragon-shifters or not, he went inside the same door Daisy had entered. As soon as he stepped inside, he was wrapped in a mixture of Dawn's and Daisy's scent, along with something faintly floral.

Daisy took his hand and tugged. "Let's start in the kitchen. You'll see how much smaller it is, although the table was the perfect size for me and Mum."

As Daisy pointed out every little thing in the kitchen, Blake took in the dishes placed on a drying rack, the towel hanging on the stove, and the other little details that truly showed him that Dawn had been yanked out of her life without warning.

Maybe if he'd seen it all the first night, right after the kiss, he might've felt guilty. But now Dawn and Daisy belonged with him. He'd always ensure that Daisy had enough room to dance where she wanted, or that Dawn could have her own desk to draw when she could snag a chance.

His dragon grunted. *Of course. They are our family now to protect and take care of.*

Daisy had just finished a story about a mug her mother had bought her from a little shop in Inverness, Scotland when Dawn, Rafe, and Jane entered the flat, too. He jumped in the first second he could and told Daisy, "All right, before we continue the tour, let's see what needs to be done, okay? Your mother can't do all the work."

She stood a little taller and nodded. "I know. I'm old enough to help now. So let's go see what she wants done."

Daisy raced back to the living room. Blake followed suit, instantly going to Dawn's side.

However, it was Jane Hartley—a human mated to the dragon-shifter named Kai—that spoke up. "So tell us what you need, Dawn. I'll make sure my brother doesn't slack off."

Rafe Hartley frowned. "You're the one who always found ways to avoid chores growing up, not me."

Jane raised her brows. "I helped Mum and Dad other ways."

Rolling his eyes, Rafe asked, "What, with charm and the ability to distract them whilst I did all the work?"

Jane shrugged. "Hey, it's not my fault you didn't think of it first."

He knew the siblings could bicker for a while, so Blake jumped in. "All that matters is that we *all* help today. Otherwise, we won't get back to Stonefire until maybe tomorrow."

Dawn spoke up. "Don't worry, there's not a lot to pack. The furniture will almost all stay here. A former colleague from my old job is going to pick it up and take it for her niece. So here's how we'll divide up the packing."

As Dawn gave the orders, Blake was amazed at how Rafe and Jane merely nodded and went to their respective tasks. He whispered for her ears only, "That pair are as stubborn and strong-willed as dragon-shifters, so I don't think you're going to have any problems with actual dragons, Dawn. It's almost like you know how to put dominance into your voice."

She smiled. "I'm just a mum, nothing more."

He wanted to kiss his mate and tell her she was so much more than that, but Daisy tugged at his shirt and asked, "Don't you want to help me with my room, Blake? I never finished my tour, and I want to show you some things before we pack them up. I have some really brilliant pictures of dragons, and a few books you guys didn't buy me. Not to mention some of my own little dragon creations. I mean, wouldn't it be brilliant to have four wings instead of two? Or imagine if you could breathe fire?"

He suspected no packing would get done for a while if Daisy had her way.

Dawn murmured, "Go. She just wants to share her life with you."

After nodding, he kissed her quickly before following Daisy into her bedroom.

And for the next thirty minutes, as he'd predicted, no actual packing took place. However, he learned more about Daisy and grew a little more confident that he could be her stepfather without too many missteps along the way. Especially once he gently nudged her to start packing, and she actually listened to him.

His crash course in fatherhood was going better than he'd ever thought possible. Maybe by the time his baby was born, he'd be ready for it.

His dragon snorted. *Babies are different. Even I know that.*

Ignoring his dragon, Blake focused on the positive and helped Daisy with whatever she needed.

Dawn watched Blake and Daisy from the doorway for a few minutes, loving how Blake was patient with all of Daisy's stories.

In her experience, most adults tried to find excuses to get away from her daughter. But Blake was making an effort, and that meant the world to her.

However, once Daisy spotted her and asked if her room was already done, Dawn went into her old bedroom and sat on the bed a second to look around her now old life.

It was mostly drawings from Daisy, pictures of them together, and a few paintings she'd done years ago.

Even though it had been only her and Daisy for so long, she could easily see more pictures of Blake with the three of them. And as she placed her hand over her lower abdomen, she smiled. It'd be four of them soon enough.

With the whirlwind of activities from the frenzy to the DDA paperwork to her mating ceremony, Dawn had rarely had a moment to think about her life changing. And yet, she didn't mind. Despite having lived in a city her entire life, she already missed Stonefire and the surrounding lakes and hills.

Which reminded her that she needed to start packing or who knew when they'd be able to go back to their new home.

Dawn didn't know how long she worked on packing up her things when Blake entered the room and immediately pulled her back against his front. He kissed her neck and murmured, "You should take a break."

Leaning into his solid chest, she smiled. "You worry

too much. As I've told you before, the pregnancy and carrying to term itself was never the problem for me, just the conceiving."

He nuzzled her cheek. "Still, I don't want to risk it."

She turned in his arms until she could loop hers around his neck. "I can't sit on a pillow for nine months, Blake. If Dr. Sid tells me to, then I'll listen. But you dragonmen have a reputation for being overprotective, and according to Evie, it's my job as your mate to keep you grounded."

He grunted. "Ask Evie how well that's worked for her with Bram."

She raised an eyebrow. "Well, this is a new side to you."

He cupped her cheek, and she barely resisted leaning into his touch. "You, Daisy, and the baby already mean so much to me, Dawn. I will always want to protect you."

As she stared into Blake's hazel eyes, it did something to her heart. He was such a contrast to her first husband's reluctance to help her out, so much so she still had trouble believing she'd snagged such a loving, kind man.

While deep down she already loved him, she was afraid to say so and jinx everything. Even if it seemed unfair since she knew Blake already loved her, Dawn just needed a little longer to convince herself it wasn't all a dream that would be snatched away at the first opportunity.

She kissed him gently and said, "How about we protect each other and our family together? That sounds like a much better idea, don't you think?"

His pupils flashed—an endearing sight to her now—

before he replied, "I guess. My dragon doesn't like it, but he's willing to try."

She bit her lip to keep from laughing at the image of Blake's dragon sulking. The dragons of myth were always so majestic, selfish, and arrogant. But in reality, they weren't all that different from humans. A bit more instinctual and protective, yes. But multi-faceted as well. "Good. Then I promise to be honest about my health as long as you don't treat me like a fragile piece of porcelain. Deal?"

He grunted. "Mostly. Just remember I can hear when your stomach rumbles, even a little, so I'm going to pester you about eating. Carrying a dragon-shifter child isn't quite the same as a human one."

A fact Dawn was learning all too quickly. "Given how I eat three times as much, I'm surprised I haven't gained a stone by now."

"You could gain ten and I wouldn't care. You'd still be my mate, and only mine."

She was about to kiss him for that when Daisy's voice filled the air. "I thought we didn't have time to play? Because if we do, then Blake is supposed to teach me that dragon-shifter card game. The one about battling dragon-shifters."

Since Dawn was facing away from Daisy, she grinned and raised her brows, telling Blake to handle that one.

He cleared his throat. "It's true, we don't have time to play right now. I was just making sure your mother wasn't too tired."

"How? I didn't think hugs or kisses would help you

figure that out. Is there a secret trick no one has taught me? Because I might need it one day."

Dawn bit her lip harder. Blake's pupils flashed a few times before he answered, "A hug can often make someone feel good, which helps even if you're tired. There's no trick to it."

"Then let me help her, too!"

Daisy raced up to them and weaseled her way to their side. Both Blake and Dawn wrapped Daisy into their three-person hug. Daisy closed her eyes and squeezed both of them.

Dawn met Blake's gaze, and they smiled at one another. In that moment, her gut said they would make a good family, one that Daisy had deserved for so long.

As soon as she could manage it—after enduring one of the longest group hugs of her life—Dawn got everyone back to work. The sooner they packed up their old life, the sooner they could truly begin their new one.

Chapter Fifteen

A week later, Blake stood at the cooker, absently stirring his sauce while Daisy did her homework at the table.

Dawn was working a little late at her new job as an assistant office manager for the Protectors, but Blake didn't mind watching Daisy. She'd received a lot of extra homework in the last few days since the teachers were trying to catch her up to the other dragon students. And Blake had secretly learned to love teaching his new daughter all about his kind.

While Daisy was far ahead of everyone else in human studies, she still had a lot to do before she could match dragon-shifter history, inner dragon studies, and dragon traditions such as dancing and ceremonies.

His dragon spoke up. *I still don't understand why she's learning about inner dragons. I wish she could have her own, but she can't.*

She may not have her own, but she needs to understand how inner dragons work or she'll never truly fit in here.

Maybe.

Daisy's voice prevented Blake from replying to his beast. "I need your help, Blake. This inner dragon cave thing is confusing. How can your dragon hide from you inside your own mind for years? I don't get it."

Setting the cooker temperature to a low simmer, he covered the pot and sat next to Daisy. Just as he was about to ask which part she was having trouble with, Dawn burst into the room. One glance at her widened eyes and he instantly knew something was wrong.

Going to her side, he stated, "Tell me what happened, Dawn."

She handed him a piece of paper. When he saw the Department of Dragon Affairs letterhead, a sense of foreboding settled over him. Since it would be faster, he read the first paragraph:

This is your official notice to appear before a DDA judge to discuss the custody of your daughter, Daisy Chadwick. A blood relative has put in a claim to take over her care. You will find a more detailed explanation as well as a copy of the filed statement from the relative enclosed in this envelope.

Someone had filed a claim to take Daisy away? He muttered, "Who the bloody hell would do that?"

Before he could shuffle through the paperwork, Dawn squeezed his bicep but looked at Daisy. "Can you go upstairs to finish your homework, love? I need to discuss something with Blake."

Daisy looked between them. Even Blake could tell she wanted to know what was going on, but they'd been working with her on the issue of privacy. Not just for them, but her, too.

With a sigh, she scooped up her book and binder. "Fine, I'll be upstairs. But only for a little while. I really do need Blake's help with my homework."

He nodded. "I'll help you as soon as I can, Daisy. I promise."

With another much more overdramatic sigh, Daisy left and trudged up the stairs. Only when he heard her walk into her room and shut the door did he focus back on Dawn. "I only read the beginning bit. But who is trying to claim Daisy? I thought her father was in Australia."

"He is. It's not him trying to claim Daisy but his sister, Susan."

Right, Susan Miller—the aunt who lived in Liverpool.

His dragon growled. *She can't have Daisy. She belongs with us. She is part of our family now.*

I know, dragon. But we have to be careful and do this the human way. Otherwise, the DDA could take her away.

His beast grumbled and curled up inside his mind, a sign for Blake to handle whatever human things needed to be done.

Guiding Dawn to a chair, he made sure she sat down before he did. "I didn't think Daisy and her aunt were that close, though?"

She shook her head. "They aren't. They usually only see each other at major holidays. But I think I've mentioned how Susan distrusts dragons, right?" He nodded, recalling a vague late-night conversation. She continued, "Well, apparently she believes Daisy living here is detrimental to her well-being. Or so her letter tries to claim." She searched his gaze. "With everything going on, I haven't really had a chance to look into it all. But it's happened before, right, a human child moving onto a dragon clan?"

What he wouldn't give to have the answers she wanted to hear. "I honestly don't know. I suspect so, but we need to talk with Evie and her friend Alice." He quickly explained how Alice Darby knew more than just about anyone when it came to dragon-shifters and every-thing about them. He continued, "But even without talking to them, just know that we'll fight this and win, Dawn. Daisy belongs here with you."

She laid a hand on his cheek. "With us, and all of Stonefire, too. She's never done so well, Blake. She's less distracted, she focuses longer than normal, and she hasn't even been in much trouble." He noticed tears welling in Dawn's eyes. "I can't lose her, Blake. I just can't."

He drew her close against his chest and held his mate. "You won't lose her, love. I promise I'm going to do what-ever it takes to win this battle."

And for a few long moments, they remained that way —silent and embracing each other as if it was the only thing keeping the world together.

Then Blake finally forced himself to release his mate long enough to call Bram and set everything up with Evie and Alice.

It seemed his life with Dawn and Daisy had been too easy so far. If he wanted a future with them, he'd have to fight for it. And Blake was more than up for the challenge.

NEARLY TWO HOURS after sharing her news with Blake, Dawn sat with him inside a meeting room on the ground floor of the Protector's main security building, waiting for Bram and the others to arrive.

Since she'd had a quick cry earlier when alone with Blake, it'd helped to clear her head a bit. The shock of the news had made Dawn forget the fact that she'd raised and taken care of Daisy all on her own for years. Daisy was Dawn's daughter, and no one else's. No one would take Daisy away from her, even if it took everything she had to keep her.

Blake squeezed her hand and she met his gaze. His reassuring, loving look helped her further push aside her fears.

Her dragonman was kind, smart, and better with Daisy than she'd hoped. Add in his sexy looks and how good he was at wringing out orgasms, and it was no wonder Dawn loved the man.

Not that she'd had a chance to tell him. However, once the custody matter was settled, she would.

The door opened and in walked Bram, Evie, and a woman with dark hair dyed blue on the ends that must be Alice Darby, Evie's friend.

They all sat across from her and Blake. It was Bram who spoke up first. "Sorry we're late. We had a few things to find out before getting here." He motioned toward the dark-haired woman. "Alice can explain it better than me. So quickly, Alice, this is Dawn and Blake. Dawn and Blake, this is Alice. Okay, now let's get down to business."

Alice leaned her arms on the table and spoke, her southern English accent similar to Evie Marshall's. "So let me get a few things out in the open. Your case isn't the first, Dawn. There have been other humans moving onto a dragon's land with their human child. However, it has been more than three decades since the last time it's happened in England."

She willed her voice to be strong as she asked, "And what happened?"

Alice answered, "The woman and her son were allowed to stay on Skyhunter. But I believe in complete honesty, so I'll tell you that the DDA was much less put together back then. Remember, the sacrifice program only really started in the late 1980s and early 1990s. The woman's case was right before that. The DDA is much stricter now since dragon-shifters are more visible in both the news and in the UK in general."

She didn't think the woman was trying to depress her, only give her honest answers. So Dawn pushed aside her sadness at how this might be much more difficult than she'd thought. She looked at each of the three people across from her in turn. "So, what do we do?"

Evie replied, "We already submitted all the necessary forms for you and Daisy to move here, and they were approved before the Susan woman filed her complaint. That works in our favor. But you'll still have to attend a hearing with you, Susan Miller, a DDA panel, and Daisy. The human social services side of things wants to leave this to the DDA, probably to avoid any association with dragons in general. You'll each state your case, and they'll talk to Daisy in private. Given how Daisy loves it here, I think she'll be your greatest asset."

She nodded. "When will it take place?"

Bram spoke up. "In a week. You'll be allowed a solicitor to help present your case. Whilst there aren't many that will represent dragon-shifters, there are a few. I have the best one coming to help you, and she should arrive tomorrow morning. Her name is Hayley Beckett. You'll meet with her at 8:00 a.m."

The last time Dawn had dealt with a solicitor had been her divorce. Why did it seem as if they were only necessary under the worst of times?

Blake spoke up. "What can I do to help? Or do I have to wait until Miss Beckett arrives?"

Bram replied, "She'll have the best advice of what you can do, but you have to prove you'll be a good father to Daisy. So it couldn't hurt to start putting everything together to prove that—finances, your job, and even references from clan members."

Blake nodded. "I'll start right after we finish here."

As Dawn looked from Blake and then to the others across the table, she felt the urge to cry again. She was barely an official clan member and they were all so willing to help her. "Thank you," she croaked.

Blake pulled her against his side as Bram waved a hand in dismissal. "Stonefire takes care of its own, which includes you. It's nothing special."

Oh, but it was, and Dawn knew it. However, she merely nodded since she didn't have enough energy to argue about something so trivial when she could possibly lose Daisy forever in the coming weeks.

No. She wouldn't let her go. With everyone at her back, they had to win. They just had to.

And as Bram, Evie, and Alice explained a few things she needed to know ahead of the custody hearing, she merely took strength from Blake's touch and did her best to keep it together. Because when she talked to Daisy about all this, she needed to be strong.

Chapter Sixteen

The next morning, Blake took Dawn and Daisy to the Protector's building for their meeting with the solicitor and tried his best not to let his mixture of anger and uneasiness show. Both of the females in his family needed strength, and he would show it.

His dragon spoke up. *Of course we'll be strong for them. Anyone who tries to take them away will have to face me.*

As much as I wish you could just shift and eat the horrible aunt, it doesn't work that way anymore.

His beast grunted. *There were some good points to the old times. Although I do prefer better hygiene and the fact people aren't constantly trying to hunt us as trophy kills. But eating our enemies was a nice touch hundreds of years ago.*

Blake resisted a sigh and focused on ushering Dawn and Daisy into the building and down the hallway.

Once they reached the correct room, he looked at Dawn and murmured, "Ready?" She nodded weakly, and he quickly kissed her forehead. "We'll win, Dawn. I know we will."

Daisy must've heard him because she asked, "What happens if we lose?"

He replied, "We're going to focus on winning. That's more important."

"Okay." Daisy stood taller. "Then let's find a way to win."

She'd taken the news the night before better than he'd expected. But Dawn had explained that Daisy was used to challenges thanks to her problems at school, and even more recently, with her former best friend.

If she was this resilient at eleven, he could only imagine what she'd be like as an adult.

Dawn turned the doorknob, and they entered the room, only to find the brown-haired, pale-skinned Hayley Beckett already sitting at the table with various piles of paper in front of her.

Her messy bun, glasses, and mismatched buttoned cardigan didn't exactly scream a high-powered solicitor, but Blake wasn't going to judge by appearance. He knew better than anyone that focusing on the way someone looked could make people focus on the wrong thing.

She smiled and stood, reaching out her hand to shake. "You must be Blake, Dawn, and Daisy. I'm Hayley Beckett, but please call me Hayley. I'd like to say nice to meet you, but it's not quite the time. So take a seat and let's get started."

Hayley shook Dawn's hand, then Blake's, and she even shook with Daisy, too.

Once they were all seated, Hayley continued. "The case is unique in that it hasn't happened in England for quite a while. However, if everything Bram told me is true, there are several points in your favor. So let's start with the basics and build up the case, okay? I need you to tell me everything about this woman who filed the complaint as well as what you've done to help Daisy adjust here."

Daisy spoke up before either Blake or Dawn could. "I can tell you some things. Like the bedroom they decorated for me. It has so many dragons, which I love, although I could always do with some more. Not to mention my new house is so close to my best friend, Freddie's. I can see him all the time now, unlike when we lived in Manchester. It's brilliant. It's almost like I'm always on holiday now."

Blake half-expected for Hayley to smile and tell Daisy to be quiet. Instead, the human asked Daisy, "What else did they do for you? Or what else do you like about living on Stonefire?"

"It's hard to remember it all! I have so many books now, new ones I didn't know existed. I also get to go to dragon school and am always surrounded by kids with flashing dragon eyes. Most of them let me ask questions. Only a few don't, but that's okay because not everyone likes me."

Blake jumped in at that. "Who?"

Daisy shrugged. "Mostly the older kids. But they don't like all my questions, or so Freddie tells me. He said that if I waited to ask questions later on, or maybe only once in a while, they'd be nicer to me. But I'm not good at holding back like that. I'm just curious is all, especially since I can never have an inner dragon and so I need to ask as many other dragon-shifters as I can. You know, just to make sure I know how it all works and stuff."

And yet, Blake still wanted to find the older children and have a chat with them.

His dragon sighed. *She'll find her position within the clan like we all do. Whilst she's fairly alpha for a human, she will never be at the top of the hierarchy. Let her find her place.*

I suppose.

Still, Blake didn't like the fact Daisy wasn't accepted by everyone.

Hopefully, Dawn could convince Daisy not to say those kinds of things during their hearing. He'd have to bring it up with her later.

For the present, he merely focused on answering Hayley's questions and taking note of what she asked them to do.

Their hearing date would come sooner than they'd like, and they had to be as prepared as possible.

LATER THAT NIGHT, after Daisy had finally fallen asleep, Dawn curled up next to Blake on their bed and laid her head on his shoulder. She sighed. "The wait for the hearing is going to kill me."

He wrapped an arm around her torso and hugged her closer. "It gives us time to prepare, love. I know we jumped into things as far as the mating and the frenzy, but the DDA is harder to please than an inner dragon or an eleven-year-old girl."

She smiled. "I suppose that's true."

As Blake rubbed her upper arm with his thumb, she snuggled more against him. After so many years of fighting everything on her own, it was comforting to have someone to lean on both literally and figuratively.

Just thinking about everything Blake had done for her and Daisy brought up the feelings she'd been trying to control.

It was time to stop hiding and be forthright. Blake deserved that much from her.

She tilted her head up and met his gaze. She said, "I love you, Blake."

His finger paused a second on her arm before resuming. He then cupped her cheek with his free hand. "I love you, too, Dawn. And at some point, I think I'll have to thank Daisy for forcing us to kiss after the play or I might've never realized how much I needed you in my life."

She maneuvered until she could straddle his lap and hold his face between her hands. As she caressed the light stubble, she murmured, "Maybe we'll wait a few years before we do that, or we'll never hear the end of it from Daisy."

He grinned, which still made her heart skip a beat even though she'd seen it more and more often lately. "She's probably already going to take credit for it."

"Yes, but let's not inflate her head too much. She's already trying to lead her entire class in some sort of effort to get them to have more shifting practice, all so she can see more dragons up close."

He chuckled and kissed her gently. "I have a feeling few people are going to say no to her, love. So you'd better get used to it."

"As long as you can say no to her—at least sometimes —then we'll be fine."

Blake threaded his fingers into her hair. "Her I can say no to. You, on the other hand, are much harder to resist."

As his pupils flashed between slits and round, a thread of heat shot through her body. Even with the enormity of the hearing looming over them, Blake could still make her temporarily forget about her problems.

And Dawn was on board for a few hours of leaving reality behind.

So she leaned forward until her lips were a hair-breadth from his and said, "Then I might just have to use that power. Because right now, I could do with a distraction."

His pupils changed quicker, and his voice was husky as he replied, "And I have no desire to deny you right now, either."

He took her lips in a kiss before she could reply, his tongue entering her mouth and exploring slowly.

Dawn caressed him back, loving how he could be slow one minute and quick the next, never knowing what Blake or his dragon would do.

In the blink of an eye, Dawn was on her back with Blake on his hands and knees above her, his pupils still flashing. "Now, all I need to know is if you want slow or quick this time."

She arched her back, eager to have her nipples rubbing against his chest. "I don't care. Just touch me, Blake. I need you."

Without another word, he shredded her clothes—why she bothered putting them on at night, she had no idea—and she waited to see what he'd do.

Even though Blake had lost count of the number of times he'd claimed Dawn since the very first time, he always craved more.

It'd been hard enough adjusting with Daisy living with them—it required being quieter than he'd like—but then they'd been thrown the custody battle, and he'd resisted taking her the night before.

So when Dawn had asked for a distraction, his guilt had fled, and he'd ripped off her clothes. His beautiful mate now lay naked below him, the scent of her arousal making his cock turn to stone.

His dragon growled. *Then do something about it. A true distraction means making her lose her mind with pleasure. If you don't give it to her, then I will.*

Not wanting to give his beast the opening, Blake lowered down until he could feel Dawn's warm, soft skin against his. Taking her lips in a quick, rough kiss, he loved how she moaned into his mouth.

Needing more than a kiss, he broke it and slowly kissed her jaw, her neck, and down to her breast. Her nipples were already straining and begging him to taste them, so Blake took one into his mouth and suckled.

Dawn arched her back and dug her nails into his scalp, a reminder of how much his mate liked for him to play with her nipples.

When he lightly nibbled, she squirmed some more. Needing to feel just how wet she was for him, he ran a hand down her side and then over to between her thighs. Lightly rubbing his finger through her folds, he growled against her breasts. She was so fucking wet already.

Moving from her nipples, he kissed between her breasts and moved to the other. As he nibbled, suckled, and licked, he also strummed her core, loving how her hips moved at his touch.

Pushing a finger inside her, Dawn cried out softly. While his mate was fairly good at keeping her voice down, he didn't want to risk it. So he released her nipple and took her mouth in a kiss before moving his finger faster.

She moved in time to his thrusts, but he soon removed his finger, and she cried out in disappointment. Releasing her lips, he murmured, "I want to torture you just a little more before you come, love."

Raising her arms above her head, she spread her legs wide. "Then don't keep me waiting."

Both man and beast mentally roared in approval. What he wouldn't give to fly her to a remote location, bend her over a log, and take her roughly, over and over again, neither of them worrying about being too loud.

His dragon roared. *Soon enough. But our female is waiting now. Don't make me take control.*

Blake ran his hands down her shoulders, lightly squeezed her breasts, and then moved them to her thighs. Spreading her wider, he settled his head between her legs and licked slowly up her slit, loving her taste. He'd never tire of her sweet honey.

Dawn managed to bite her lip to keep from making noise, which encouraged him to do it again, and then once more. It was only then he lightly circled her clit, and Dawn bucked her hips.

He lightly rubbed and flicked her tight bud as he thrust one finger inside her, and then soon two. Even though he was pleasing her, the sight of her grabbing the sheets and arching her back made his cock even harder.

He'd be claiming her more than once during the night, that was for sure.

As he increased the flicks of his tongue, her face and neck flushed more, telling him she was close. Knowing what to do by now having learned many of her desires, he lightly suckled her clit as he thrust his fingers harder. Dawn groaned and then stilled as she sucked in a breath.

Her pussy milked his fingers, and Blake removed them so he could lap at her orgasm, knowing full well the quick flicks against her entrance would only make her come harder.

Once Dawn relaxed against the bed with a sigh, his dragon growled. *Now it's my turn.*

Allowing his beast to take over, Blake retreated as his dragon flipped Dawn over and said, "You're mine, human. Let me remind you."

Then his dragon thrust their cock into Dawn and

took her quick and rough, Dawn doing her best not to make loud noises the whole time.

And so it went for another hour and a half, man and beast taking turns with their mate, helping her to forget about the outside world for at least a little while.

Chapter Seventeen

After the longest two weeks of her life, Dawn finally looked up at the brick and glass building that contained the Department of Dragon Affairs branch in Manchester and willed for the day to go her way.

Not that she had long to think about it because Daisy tugged her hand and asked, "Are we going to go on a tour first? I've never been inside, and I always wonder if the DDA has some special dragon stuff they keep hidden from everyone else. You know, paintings and old jewelry or something, that we can see only if we ask nicely."

She smiled at Daisy's enthusiasm. "It's not a museum, Daisy. And our appointment is in twenty minutes, which isn't enough time for a tour. And no, not even a quick one, before you ask."

Daisy slumped her shoulders. "Okay. Maybe later, though? I can at least ask if they give them. And if they say there's nothing to show me, then I can ask why not. Maybe they need to open a museum to help people like dragon-shifters more. I bet my old classmates would love it, and maybe it'd make them less afraid. It really is a brilliant idea."

Blake squeezed Dawn's other hand, and she shared an amused glance with her mate. Dawn replied to Daisy, "Maybe there is someone we can set up an appointment with, so you can ask some questions later but not today. Remember, we all need to be on our best behavior and tell the DDA people whatever they need to know."

Daisy bobbed her head. "I know that. I even brought my list of things I like about Stonefire, just in case I forget some and they need more reasons."

Dawn had seen the list, complete with over two hundred points, and didn't think the DDA panel would need that many reasons. But she had to give her daughter credit for being well-prepared.

Blake spoke up. "We should head inside. It's always better to be early than late."

Even though the sound of people walking around, the tram in the distance, or even just the car horns probably drove Blake and his dragon mad, he was calm and collected on the surface.

He was enduring something he disliked so much for her and Daisy.

It made her love him even more.

She gently pushed Daisy. "Let's go. Maybe you can look over your list again while we wait, to make sure you're extra prepared."

Which would keep her daughter occupied for a while, meaning she wouldn't irritate the DDA employees in whatever waiting room they were shuffled into. While

Dawn thought Daisy had a great idea about opening museums related to dragon-shifters—a visual way to educate people—now wasn't the time to bring it up or risk irritating someone who could decide their fate.

After checking in with reception, they rode the lift to the second floor and went down the hall to the door that read, "DDA Hearings and Deliberations." The person at the desk inside the door showed them to a waiting room, also telling them that their solicitor, Hayley Beckett, would join them inside the deliberation room right before it started.

As Daisy went over her list, occasionally asking if she should add some more details, Dawn sat next to Blake, his hand in hers, and took strength from his calm presence. Her life could be decided in a matter of minutes. And no matter how resolved or determined she was, the upcoming meeting could throw a huge wrench into her life.

~

BLAKE TRIED to relax his mate by rubbing circles on the back of her hand with his thumb. However, she remained tense.

His dragon sighed. *Of course she is. If they take Daisy away, it'll destroy her.*

Especially since it wasn't as if Dawn could just leave and go back to her old life. She carried a dragon-shifter child, and once it was born, he or she would have to live on Stonefire. Which meant Dawn would either have to leave the child with him and move back to Manchester with Daisy or leave Daisy in the care of her aunt and raise her new baby.

It was rather an impossible choice.

Not that he wanted to think of it. They'd come prepared, had as much knowledge as they could to face it, and Daisy's enthusiasm for Stonefire should help in their favor.

Altogether, it had to give him and Dawn the outcome they wanted.

His dragon said softly, *Maybe. The DDA has improved in the last few years, but nothing is guaranteed with them.*

You say that, but the DDA Director, Rosalind Abbott, owes Stonefire for bringing down the Dragon Knights. Maybe Bram called in that favor.

I don't know if she has that reach or will deign to interfere in the lower ranks of the department.

Before Blake could reply, a human employee walked up to them. "It's time. Follow me."

They made their way out of the waiting room and down the hall into a much bigger chamber. Blake barely paid attention to the furnishings or the like because he noticed two things at the same time—Hayley was sitting at one table and two humans at another. One of the humans was the aunt in question.

His beast growled. *I wish she'd look this way. Then we could flash our eyes and scare her a little.*

As much as I want to do that, too, we probably shouldn't stir up any trouble. The staff will take notice of every little thing we do.

His dragon huffed. *Stupid human ways I'll never understand.*

They all sat down next to Hayley, with Daisy between

him and Dawn. Hayley turned and whispered, "Just do as we discussed and it should be fine."

It was the "should" part of her sentence he didn't like.

Daisy took his hand with one of hers and her mother's with the other. She stated, "We'll win, remember?"

Even though the aunt didn't look at them, Blake noticed her frown. Clearly she didn't understand just how much Daisy loved dragon-shifters.

No, the female just wanted to win against the dragons and display how much she hated them. No matter what Stonefire or the other dragon clans did would ever change that.

His beast said, *Her loss. And as long as she doesn't try to kill some of us, just ignore her.*

He had a hard time believing the short woman would be able to orchestrate an assassination hit, let alone do it herself.

A door opened at the far side and a group of humans —two females and three males—walked in and took their place at the long table at the front of the room.

One of the females sat in the middle and spoke first. "Today we're here to discuss full custody of Daisy Chadwick. The parties are her mother, Dawn Chadwick, and her paternal aunt, Susan Miller. Statements have been submitted by both parties, but today's meeting will factor even more in our final decision. Right, then let's begin."

And so for the next twenty minutes, the two solicitors walked through each of their cases. Blake didn't follow the particulars of the law very closely, but Dawn used being her mother and caring for her on her own for nearly a decade as her defense. The aunt's reasoning was that a human girl should be raised in the human world.

The questions were so boring that even Blake's dragon fell asleep for awhile.

However, he remained awake and continued to give support to his female and new daughter when needed. His participation was limited, which seemed odd considering Daisy would be living with both him and Dawn.

That could mean the female leading the questioning didn't think highly of dragon-shifters.

But Blake lived by trial and error, facts, and numbers. So he pushed aside any speculation and merely answered when necessary. If the decision turned out negatively, he would help formulate a new plan. Because both man and beast needed to ensure their mate could be happy. And Dawn would never be happy without Daisy.

So he waited for the end of the hearing, when they could maybe have a better idea of what their future would be.

IT TOOK every bit of strength Dawn possessed to remain calm and not start pacing the room. Susan had no problem sitting there calmly, answering questions. Of course she merely saw Daisy as a pawn for her beliefs, not the key to her happiness.

True, Susan probably cared a little for Daisy. But seeing as Susan had been fine with seeing Daisy once or maybe twice a year before this whole debacle, Dawn doubted the proceedings and battle were done out of love.

Having Daisy sit next to her helped more than anything, as did occasional foot touches from Blake. Not to mention that despite Hayley's slightly disheveled appearance from their first meeting, the woman was persistent and sharp for the proceedings.

After nearly an hour, the woman in charge pointed toward Daisy. "And now, are you ready for some questions, Daisy?"

Daisy sat up a little straighter. Never the shy one, she bobbed her head and said, "Yes, ma'am. I'm ready."

Dawn smiled at Daisy's formality.

The woman in charge was named Ms. Cook, and her voice was a tad less stern when she asked Daisy, "If given the choice, would you want to go back to your old school or stay at your new one?"

"Oh, my new one. My best friend, Freddie, is there, and I've been making other friends, too. Not to mention they're all dragon-shifters, and so that means I can see them in their dragon forms during practice time. Even though I can't shift, Mr. MacLeod helps teach me some other things, since I'm behind."

Ms. Cook asked, "Don't you miss your human friends?"

"Well, I do miss Emily. But she loves dragons, too. Especially since she made a new friend named Jayden. She'll visit us loads, I'm sure. So it's not too bad."

The woman asked another question. "Some people won't like you because you live with the dragons. There are dragon hunters and they sometimes kill humans who like dragons. Are you afraid?"

Dawn opened her mouth to protest—why would they ask a child about being murdered—but Hayley placed a hand on her arm and gave a minuscule shake of her head. Apparently, Dawn needed to allow the question.

Clenching her jaw closed, she waited to see how Daisy answered. Her daughter tapped her chin a second and then replied, "No, I don't think so. Bram and Kai and Nikki and everyone works so hard to keep us safe. And they told me that I'm part of the clan now, too. So they'll do everything to keep me safe, too. Plus, I learned loads about dragon and human wars in school recently. So it's happened over and over again in history and humans are still okay. I think that means it'll always happen, right? As long as people hate dragons for just being dragons. Or something like that."

Ms. Cook nodded. "Probably. I have one more question for you, Daisy. Everyone is nice to you right now on Stonefire, but that could change. What if there was a new war against humans and everyone started to hate you? Wouldn't you want to move away?"

Dawn bit her lip to keep from telling the woman off. Some of her questions weren't appropriate for a child.

But leave it to Daisy to just shrug and say, "Not really. I mean, I've heard lots of bad things about dragons, and that didn't stop me from wanting to see them. And now my best friend is a dragon-shifter. Freddie would never hate me. And I don't think his mum, or Bram, or the others would, either. There are lots of human mates, too.

Even dragon-shifters would see that not all humans are bad."

Oh, Daisy. Her daughter was insightful without even trying.

"Perhaps," Ms. Cook murmured. Then she looked at each of the adults in turn. "We have everything we need. We'll send our verdict in the next week."

With that, the panel filed out of the room. And without even glancing their way—not even at Daisy— Susan and her solicitor exited, too.

Anger churned in Dawn's stomach. The bloody woman just wanted to use Daisy to make a statement. And if the panel decided to hand over her daughter to Susan, Dawn would have to think about snatching Daisy back and flee into hiding.

Hayley's voice broke through her rescue planning. "I'd like to go over how I think it'll go from here. Let's find some lunch, and I can answer any of your questions."

Daisy chimed in. "But can I ask about dragon museums on our way out? I don't want to forget, and it's something they really should know about. I mean, if they don't exist already, of course. But if not, they should."

Smiling, Dawn nodded. "Okay, but only for a minute or so, and then we're off to lunch. Agreed?"

"Okay." Daisy stood and rushed to the door. "Let's go!"

Dawn stood, and Blake moved instantly to her side. He kissed her and murmured, "Daisy's portion went quite well."

She watched Daisy stop at the doorway and jog in

place, trying to hurry them up. "It did, and it gives me hope."

He pulled her against his side and turned them toward the door. "For now, let's learn all we can, get some lunch, and I may just reveal the surprise I have in store for you this week."

She raised her brows at Blake. "A surprise?"

He smiled. "Yes, a surprise. And I only mentioned it once Daisy was out of earshot because otherwise, it wouldn't be a surprise for long. She'd get it out of me in no time."

She snorted. "Very true." Searching Blake's eyes, she touched his cheek. "I love you."

"I love you, too."

Hayley cleared her throat. "We should go before the next appointment enters the room."

And so with great effort, Dawn followed Blake's lead and did her best to be positive for Daisy for the rest of the day.

Chapter Eighteen

A few days later, Blake looked over the packed lunches on the kitchen counter and nodded to himself. Even for his pregnant mate, there should be enough food for the afternoon.

His dragon spoke up. *If she's still hungry, she can have some of ours.*

Daisy raced into the kitchen and skidded to a halt next to him. "Can we go yet? I'm ready, and so is Mum. If we leave right away, that means we'll have more time for your surprise. And since you had to pack lunches, it means it's not on Stonefire. Right?"

He smiled. "That is a long-winded way to say you want to see my dragon."

"Well, of course, I haven't really seen him much, and it's not just me. Mum likes him, too. And with the sun? You'll be all sparkly."

His dragon grunted. *We do not sparkle.*

You do, a bit.

His dragon huffed and fell silent.

Before Daisy could ask what his dragon said—she still did that all the time, despite the gentle reminders about how you shouldn't do that with dragon-shifters—he handed her some of the packed lunches. "Take these to the car. I'll carry the rest, and then we can go."

Without another word, Daisy grabbed her share of the lunches and raced out of the room.

His dragon said, *At least she's not thinking about the custody trial.*

There still hadn't been any word yet. Dawn had a hard time sleeping, and it made both man and beast anxious. *Today will hopefully distract her. After all, she said her perfect day would be sunny and outside.*

Too bad it's not very warm.

Well, we do what we can, considering this is the North of England.

Daisy yelled from the front door, "Do you need more help, Blake? Mum's waiting in the car now, too."

Shaking his head at how skillfully Daisy could make someone feel guilty with a few words, he scooped up the remaining lunch things and went to join his mate and daughter.

Since Blake had never learned to drive, he slid into the passenger's side and shut the door. Dawn raised her brows. "Well, since you won't tell me where we're going, I need some sort of direction to get started."

Even if he didn't drive, Blake had flown the route many times over and had taken note of the roads below. So he gave directions to get them going, and continued to give Dawn further ones until they reached a peaceful valley surrounded by hills.

As soon as Dawn pulled into a turnout spot, he said, "We'll leave the lunches here for now. But bring the blankets and towels."

Dawn raised her brows. "It's not exactly warm."

"Just trust me, love."

"Okay," she said as she exited the car and helped take out what was needed from the trunk.

Blake guided them down a pathway until they came to the shore of a small lake. He gestured toward it. "This is my favorite place to swim in the lake. I thought I'd show you my dragon form and go for a swim." He winked and leaned to Dawn's ear so that only she could hear. "Although you'll have to wait for me to shift between human and dragon since Daisy's here."

She lightly hit his arm. "Considering how cold it is, I'm not sure you'd want to do that right now anyway. It'll be a little less impressive, won't it?"

"Cheeky female," he murmured before he kissed her lips briefly.

Right on cue, Daisy jumped on the silence. "When will you shift, Blake? I really want to see your dragon, and help scratch your ears, and maybe you'll even let me sit on your back? None of the other adults will let me do that, and it's a pain even with Freddie most of the time. So you have to let me do it, just to see what it's like to be that tall."

Giving Dawn one last kiss, he faced his stepdaughter. "Set the blankets on the ground and turn away. Only then will I shift."

Daisy tossed the blanket on the ground, not caring if it was laid flat, and plopped herself down, her back to him. "Ready!"

He chuckled and slowly shed his clothes. After touching Dawn's cheek one last time, he moved far enough away to change forms.

His wings sprouted from his back, his legs and arms grew, and his face elongated into a snout. In less than a minute, he stood in his white dragon form.

Giving a small growl, he let his family know he was done.

Daisy was up and at his side within seconds. She patted his scales. "You're so shiny, Blake. You really do sparkle, more than the other dragons."

Dawn bit her lip to keep from laughing.

However, Daisy went along his side and back to his tail. She shouted, "There it is! Everyone mentions your spot, but it's not really that big, is it? Or that special. I mean, it doesn't sparkle as much as your white scales. So I don't know what everyone goes on about it."

And as she touched his spot, Blake didn't tense up or feel the need to run away. Dawn and Daisy were his family now, and he wanted to share this part of him with them.

His dragon spoke up. *Maybe now you'll not care if everyone else thinks the bloody spot is special.*

With time, yes. After all, once the baby is born and grows up a little, we'll have to help him or her with shifting. And when that time comes, helping our child will be more important than a few bystanders.

Good. Although I hope it doesn't take that long. I'd like to fly more and shift without worrying about if the landing area is empty or not.

Dawn came up to him, interrupting his conversation with his dragon, and he lowered his head. She didn't waste time scratching behind his ears.

Daisy soon joined in and even convinced him to lay down so she could climb on his back.

The next hour or so flew by, all of them forgetting about what could happen in the future. Right then, they cared about having fun and making a memory for their new family. Nothing else mattered.

DAWN KNEW that Blake had planned the day to distract her, and it worked.

He'd remembered their silly speed dating event and her answer about her perfect day. True, it wasn't as warm as she'd like, but as Daisy squealed when Blake jumped into the lake in his dragon form, it was even better than she could've imagined.

While still new, they were a family. One that she didn't want to ever let go.

She watched Blake do various stunts in the water, tackling most of Daisy's request, and couldn't help but laugh.

She had no idea of how much time had passed when another dragon came into sight. Dawn wasn't good enough to tell who the purple beast was, but they landed, folded their wings, and looked between Blake, Daisy, and back again.

Blake nudged Daisy toward Dawn, and she understood what they wanted. The purple dragon needed to shift, and unless Dawn was comfortable with Daisy being around two naked adults, Daisy needed to look away.

While Dawn knew eventually she'd have to be comfortable with the idea of naked strangers because of shifting and her own half-dragon child, she wasn't quite there yet. So she went to Daisy and turned them away from the pair as she said, "Let them shift so Blake can see what the purple dragon wants."

"I bet it's Nikki. She likes to do that extra wing flutter when she lands."

Dawn brushed some hair from Daisy's face. "You really do notice everything when it comes to dragon-shifters, don't you?"

"Of course. They don't all look alike, even though people say that. Just like humans, they have small differences."

Blake's voice prevented her from replying, "Come here, Dawn and Daisy. Nikki had some news."

When they turned around, Dawn noticed Nikki was already in her dragon form again. The woman was fast.

As she hurried Daisy to Blake, she noticed he had his trousers on, but nothing else. Normally she'd appreciate the water dripping down his chest, but she was more interested in the news at the moment. "What is it?"

He took her hand and Daisy's. "The DDA has decided Daisy can stay with Stonefire provided they have regular check-ins and allow her aunt to see her a few times a year."

Dawn wanted nothing to do with Susan, but she'd take that over losing Daisy forever.

Hugging her daughter to her side, she said, "You're staying with me, Daisy."

"Not just you, but all of us. We're a family, right? Blake said he wouldn't leave, and I don't have to leave, so we can stay together and be a family."

Dawn smiled. "Yes, we can." As she hugged Daisy to her side, she met Blake's gaze and tried her best to blink away her tears. "But this is just our starter family. We'll grow and have more to love soon enough."

Daisy spoke up again. "That will be brilliant. Well, as long as I don't have to babysit all the time. But just think —I can see his or her little dragon first. And help my brother or sister learn how to be a dragon. I know I'm not one, but if I study hard, I can help. That's what big sisters do."

"Yes, they do."

And as Daisy went on about all the things she wanted to learn and teach her new sibling, Dawn merely smiled at Blake and conveyed with her eyes how happy she was. Not only would she have her daughter with her, but she also had a second chance at life with Blake and their new baby.

Dawn had never been happier and looked forward to whatever the future might bring.

Epilogue

20 Months Later

Dawn watched as Blake and Daisy tried to put the little party hats on her twin boys. Except, when one would get it on Jasper, then Theo would knock his off. And then vice versa.

Still, the fact Blake and Daisy would keep trying just so she could get the perfect picture warmed her heart.

While the twins' first birthday was special on its own, there was another reason Daisy and Blake were trying so hard. After all, in a few months, they'd have another child to join the family, too, and they wanted to spoil all three of their current children up until the last minute.

She resisted placing a hand on her belly since she needed both for her phone. However, while dragon-shifter population skewed male, Dawn secretly hoped she could have another daughter.

Daisy and Blake finally managed to get the hats on and quickly stepped to the side. Daisy shouted, "Now, Mum!"

And so she snapped a few pictures with her phone before the hats ended up on the floor again.

Laughing, she walked toward her boys. "Hey, you two should be happy. Daisy wanted hats with extra glitter and feathers on them."

Daisy jumped in. "Well, I wasn't sure how to make dragon wings, exactly. And then Blake said they'd be too pointy and sharp anyway, so I really did compromise."

Her daughter was nearly thirteen, and yet, Dawn was always surprised at how much more grown up she sounded by the day. Hugging Daisy to her side, she replied, "The hats look fabulous, Daisy-love. It's almost like a mini-aquarium on each one."

"Well, Jasper and Theo like it when Blake swims in the lake in his dragon form. And a lake was too big to fit on a hat, not to mention the fish are more interesting in the sea, so I just went with my imagination."

Blake pulled one of the cupcakes just out of reach of Jasper. "I think we'd better light the candles now or there won't be any cupcakes to use for singing 'Happy Birthday.'"

Dawn snorted. "Dragon-shifter boys *do* eat a lot." She placed a hand on her protruding belly. "If this is a boy, too, then we may need a bigger kitchen if we're to feed them all."

Daisy jumped in. "I still say you should just find out

now, Mum. The waiting would kill me if I were pregnant."

She tilted her head. "It's dragon-shifter tradition, Daisy. I thought you'd be excited we're following it?"

Her daughter frowned. "Usually, yes. But waiting nearly nine months is just too long."

Dawn laughed and released her daughter to help Blake with the cupcakes. "Just be grateful you aren't a dragon-shifter, then, because you'd have to wait six or seven years to meet your inner dragon."

"I suppose. But I can't remember much from when I was that little. So I'm guessing it's not as difficult as when you're older."

Blake grunted. "It depends. I have some things I've been testing for years now and still haven't figured out."

Daisy shook her head. "I couldn't wait that long! I guess I can't be a scientist, then."

Jasper leaned forward and managed to reach the edge of the cupcake. Dawn clapped her hands and said, "We'll talk about patience later. Right now, let's light the candles and sing 'Happy Birthday.'"

Blake lit the candles and as the three of them sang 'Happy Birthday' to Jasper and Theo, Dawn couldn't stop smiling. And not just because she had the bigger family she had always wanted.

There was going to be an even bigger party later in the day, with Sasha and some of the other mums and children. Dawn had gone from being on her own with Daisy to having a loving mate, more children, and more friends than she could count.

And all because of an accidental kiss nearly two years

ago. Her second chance had started out with a bang, and Dawn was determined to keep her happy ending for the rest of her life.

Author's Note

This story is one I hadn't really planned on writing. However, so many people asked about Dawn and Blake after reading my short story, *The Dragon Play*, that it made me wonder if I should tell it. And then I couldn't stop thinking about them and decided a short novel would be a good fit for their story. There's not as much angst or drama, and yet their story deserved to be told, too. It also introduces Daisy Chadwick to my main Stonefire readers. She's important and will play a big role in the Stonefire Dragons Legacy series I have planned for when all the kids are grown up. (I have to finish this timeline, first!) She will help with a monumental change in the human-dragon world down the line.

Curious yet?

The next Stonefire story will feature Hayley Beckett (the solicitor/lawyer in *Treasured*) and Nathan Woodhouse (IT dragonman you've met a few times in the series), but I need to write at least one (or maybe two) more in the

Lochguard series first. I will definitely write *The Dragon Collective* (Lochguard #8) in 2021, about Cat and Lachlan. As for the rest, make sure to join my newsletter to keep up-to-date on upcoming releases!

As always, there are some people I'd like to thank for their help with getting this book out into the world:

● Becky Johnson and her team at Hot Tree Editing. Becky always catches the little things, and even after all these years, she still makes me a better writer.

● Iliana G., Donna H., Sabrina D., and Sandy H. are my fantastic beta-readers and they catch the lingering typos and inconsistencies. Thanks to all my wonderful betas.

And lastly, thanks to you, the reader. You make my dream job a reality! Here's to hoping you follow along for many more books to come. I'll see you at the end of the next story!

Turn the page for a look at the first book in my American dragon-shifter series, *The Dragon's Choice*.

The Dragon's Choice

TAHOE DRAGON MATES #1

After Jose Santos's younger sister secretly enters them both into the yearly dragon lottery and they get selected, he begrudgingly agrees to participate. It means picking a human female from a giant room full of them and staying around just long enough to get her pregnant. However, when his dragon notices one female who keeps hiding behind a book, Jose has a new plan—win his fated mate, no matter what it takes.

Victoria Lewis prefers being home with a book and away from large crowds. But she desperately wants to study dragon-shifters at close range, so she musters up her courage to enter the dragon lottery. When she's selected as one of the potential candidates, she decides to accept her spot. After all, it's not as if the dragon-shifter will pick her—an introverted bookworm who prefers jeans and sweats to skirts or fancy clothes. Well, until he's standing right in front of her with flashing eyes and says he wants her.

As Jose tries to win his fated female, trouble stirs inside his clan. Will he be able to keep his mate with him forever? Or will the American Department of Dragon Affairs whisk her away to some other clan to protect her?

NOTE: This is a quick, steamy standalone story about fated mates and sexy dragon-shifters near Lake Tahoe in the USA. You don't have to read all my other dragon books to enjoy this one!

∼

Chapter One

Jose Santos waited inside a small room, one adjacent to the ballroom of the human hotel, and resisted the urge to run.

He'd never understood why people wanted to live cheek and jowl among thousands, with concrete and pavement covering the ground and banishing most of nature. Despite having worked with the humans in the US Forest Service for over a decade, he still barely understood them.

And yet here he was, inside a hotel in South Lake Tahoe, about ready to pick a human female at random to hopefully impregnate and increase his kind.

His inner dragon—the second personality inside his

head—spoke up. *Remember, you can't fuck this up today or you'll dash Gaby's dreams.*

Ah, yes. Gabriela, the little sister who had entered them both into the yearly lottery, one she couldn't enter herself since it had to be all the unmated siblings in a family or nothing. *Considering she didn't ask my permission, I'm being pretty fucking generous just being here.*

You had the chance to back out last month, but you didn't. And we both know why.

Damn dragon, knowing too much.

Every dragon-shifter lived to find their true mate, the one that stirred their inner beast and kicked off a mate-claim frenzy when kissed.

However, despite the millions of visitors that came to the greater Lake Tahoe area every year, Jose had never so much as glimpsed at a female who urged him to do more than growl and tell them to leave him the hell alone.

He had no tolerance for the dragon groupies that came to the lake to try to find a dragon-shifter to kiss or fuck. Entire tourist companies had grown around such a goal. He was surprised the human government hadn't stepped in to intervene, especially since, in recent years, it'd forced most of the dragon clans in the area to keep more and more to themselves to avoid the hassle.

Not that dealing with the groupies was his problem to solve. Jose only wanted the chance to spot his true mate, and this lottery gave him a chance to really look at a group of humans without having to run and avoid females throwing themselves at him.

His inner dragon snorted. *That one who jumped off a*

boat, to try and land on us as we floated in the lake, deserved some points for originality.

No, it was pure stupidity. She couldn't swim, and we had to save her. And we're not the only ones who've had to dodge them like bullets.

His beast huffed. *Well, you can't complain too much about today, then. The rules won't allow the females to run or jump on us.*

Which is the only reason I'm here.

True, while the chances of her being inside the next room were slim to say the least, it was worth the time to look, even if his true mate ended up being human, which wasn't his first choice.

And even if she wasn't here, then he should at least get a few fun fucks out of it—ones where he controlled the situation—so it wasn't a complete loss.

An employee from the American Department of Dragon Affairs—or ADDA—barged into the room. Even though the female was short and would probably blow over if Jose breathed too hard, she stood tall and didn't wither at his hard expression. Good thing, too, as these lotteries tended to work better when the humans in charge weren't afraid.

He'd met her once before and knew her name was Ashley Swift. The human motioned with her hand. "Come on. It's time to get this thing started."

Not moving, Jose asked, "How many are there?"

"About two hundred or so candidates passed the interviews and tests this time."

Two hundred lucky ones, at least according to the humans. Every few years, they held these lotteries in South

Lake Tahoe for the surrounding dragon clans, and every time thousands entered. Not all dragon clans in the US were as open to mating or reproducing with humans, but the four Tahoe area clans preferred survival over purity.

Jose rolled his shoulders. "All right, let's do this."

Ashley raised her brows. "You remember the rules, right?"

He sighed. "Of course I do. She has to come willingly, and no kissing until she signs the paperwork. All pretty fucking romantic, isn't it?"

Ashley didn't blink an eye. "Getting her to be willing may be hard for you, Mr. Santos, if you don't at least try to be less intimidating."

He eyed the slip of a woman and leaned close. "Are you sure you don't want to enter?"

She rolled her eyes. "My fiancé would definitely have a word or two to say about that suggestion."

Damn, of course the one human female who didn't treat him like some god would already belong to another. Now if he could just find one like her but unattached, he might actually not dread this.

His dragon murmured, *Plenty exist. Our cousin's friend mated one.*

Yes, but that was in Canada where dragons and humans have much longer histories of understanding and cooperation than in the US.

Ashley turned toward the door. "It's now or never, Mr. Santos. This is the last chance to back out, but it will pull your sister out, too, and disqualify your clan from entering for five years."

Which would mean Gaby wouldn't have her stupid fantasy come true next month.

Jose may be cynical, but he loved his younger sister. So he took a step toward the door, kicking the ADDA employee into motion, and they both entered the ballroom.

Curious about what happens next? *The Dragon's Choice* is available in paperback.

The Conquest

KELDERAN RUNIC WARRIORS #1

Leader of a human colony planet, Taryn Demara has much more on her plate than maintaining peace or ensuring her people have enough to eat. Due to a virus that affects male embryos in the womb, there is a shortage of men. For decades, her people have enticed ships to their planet and tricked the men into staying. However, a ship hasn't been spotted in eight years. So when the blip finally shows on the radar, Taryn is determined to conquer the newcomers at any cost to ensure her people's survival.

Prince Kason tro el Vallen needs to find a suitable planet for his people to colonize. The Kelderans are running out of options despite the fact one is staring them in the face —Planet Jasvar. Because a group of Kelderan scientists disappeared there a decade ago never to return, his people dismiss the planet as cursed. But Kason doesn't believe in curses and takes on the mission to explore the planet to prove it. As his ship approaches Jasvar, a distress signal chimes in and Kason takes a group down to the planet's surface to explore. What he didn't expect was for a band of females to try and capture him.

As Taryn and Kason measure up and try to outsmart each other, they soon realize they've found their match. The only question is whether they ignore the spark between them and focus on their respective people's survival or can they find a path where they both succeed?

The Conquest is available in paperback.

Also by Jessie Donovan

Asylums for Magical Threats

Blaze of Secrets (AMT #1)

Frozen Desires (AMT #2)

Shadow of Temptation (AMT #3)

Flare of Promise (AMT #4)

Cascade Shifters

Convincing the Cougar (CS #0.5)

Reclaiming the Wolf (CS #1)

Cougar's First Christmas (CS #2)

Resisting the Cougar (CS #3)

Kelderan Runic Warriors

The Conquest (KRW #1)

The Barren (KRW #2)

The Heir (KRW #3)

The Forbidden (KRW #4)

The Hidden (KRW #5)

The Survivor / Kajala Mayven (KRW #6 / 2021)

Lochguard Highland Dragons

The Dragon's Dilemma (LHD #1)

The Dragon Guardian (LHD #2)

The Dragon's Heart (LHD #3)

The Dragon Warrior (LHD #4)

The Dragon Family (LHD #5)

The Dragon's Discovery (LHD #6)

The Dragon's Pursuit (LHD #7)

The Dragon Collective / Cat & Lachlan (LHD #8 / 2021)

Love in Scotland

Crazy Scottish Love (LiS #1)

Chaotic Scottish Wedding (LiS #2)

Stonefire Dragons

Sacrificed to the Dragon (SD #1)

Seducing the Dragon (SD #2)

Revealing the Dragons (SD #3)

Healed by the Dragon (SD #4)

Reawakening the Dragon (SD #5)

Loved by the Dragon (SD #6)

Surrendering to the Dragon (SD #7)

Cured by the Dragon (SD #8)

Aiding the Dragon (SD #9)

Finding the Dragon (SD #10)

Craved by the Dragon (SD #11)

Persuading the Dragon (SD #12)

Treasured by the Dragon (SD #13)

Captivating the Dragon / Hayley & Nathan (SD #14, TBD)

Stonefire Dragons Shorts

Meeting the Humans (SDS #1)

The Dragon Camp (SDS #2)

The Dragon Play (SDS #3)

Stonefire Dragons Universe

Winning Skyhunter (SDU #1)

Transforming Snowridge (SDU #2)

Tahoe Dragon Mates

The Dragon's Choice (TDM #1)

The Dragon's Need (TDM #2)

The Dragon's Bidder (TDM #3)

The Dragon's Charge (TDM #4 / Nov 2020)

The Dragon's Weakness (TDM #5 / 2021)

WRITING AS LIZZIE ENGLAND

Her Fantasy

Holt: The CEO

Callan: The Highlander

Adam: The Duke

Gabe: The Rock Star

About the Author

Jessie Donovan has sold over half a million books, has given away hundreds of thousands more to readers for free, and has even hit the *NY Times* and *USA Today* best-seller lists. She is best known for her dragon-shifter series, but also writes about elemental magic users, alien warriors, and even has a crazy romantic comedy series set in Scotland. When not reading a book, attempting to tame her yard, or traipsing around some foreign country on a shoestring, she can often be found interacting with her readers on Facebook. She lives near Seattle, where, yes, it rains a lot but it also makes everything green.

Visit her website at: www.JessieDonovan.com

Printed in Great Britain
by Amazon